I0523730

Chasing THE Storm

Jessica Madden

Copyrighted © 2025 Violet Hearts Publishing

First published 2018

All rights reserved.

The right of Jessica Madden to be identified as the Author of the Work has been asserted by her in accordance with the Copyright, Designs and Patents Act 1988.

All rights reserved. No part of this publication may be reproduced, stored in a retrieval system, or transmitted, in any form or by any means without the prior written permission of the Publisher, nor be otherwise circulated in any form of binding or cover other than that in which it is published and without a similar condition being imposed on the subsequent purchaser.

All characters in this publication are fictional and any resemblance to real persons, living or dead is purely coincidental.

Cover design by Amygdala design

ISBN: 9780646710846

For my niece, Sophie

Prologue

Everything started out as a normal day. A clear, humid summer's day. And then the clouds started rolling in for an afternoon thunderstorm.

But it was no ordinary thunderstorm.

There was no warning for the approaching tornado. No sirens at all to warn us to get to safety. Australia didn't have those kind of emergency warnings for tornadoes. The only warning we had was the sound of the roaring freight train.

The hotel staff run around the lobby, unsure what to do as they scramble to get people on the ground floor to take shelter. With the power out, the manager is unable to alert the ones who weren't in the lobby. No one is prepared for this, or trained to know what to do during a tornado. There is no safe place for us to take cover. Not in the little time we have. We follow staff orders to stay away from doors and windows, crouch down against the wall, covering our heads and hope for the best.

I stay close to my parents as we huddle together with other guests staying at this hotel. I'm in the middle of my parents, my dad telling both Mum and I that everything will be okay. No one speaks, except a few younger kids saying how scared they were, waiting for the tornado to hit us. The panic in this room made it hard to breathe.

The sound of debris is heard as they thump, scrape and slam against the building as the funnel cloud gets closer. And then the glass shatters. What was a silence filled room was now filled with a roar. The air is suck out, and I'm unable to breathe. Nails rip out of the walls, tearing apart the floors above us. Objects shatter as they are used as missiles. Screams of terror are heard over the loud whooping and roaring noise. My own screams drown in the noise.

I squeeze my eyes shut, wanting this to be all over, something hits my back a throbbing pain shooting up my spine. The wind tugs on me, threatening to pull me along. I hold on tightly to my dad as my knuckles turn to white, my hand hurting from gripping so hard. I loosen my grip a little to ease the pain, but only to hold tighter again as the power of the wind pulls on me. Its strength was much stronger than me that I feel myself slipping from my mother's grip.

And then the wind stops.

Chapter 1

Six years later

The plane lands on the tarmac of Kansas City Airport. I rarely pay any attention to the scenery outside my window, except for the clouds. They are a charcoal colour, looking as if it may rain at any second. I didn't mind the rain. It was storms I loathed. On my last layover before coming here, I made sure to check the weather. Thankfully around Missouri, where my mother said she will meet me, wasn't expecting any storms today. Just an overcast day with possible rain.

Once I'm off the plane and head to baggage claim, I only have to wait for a few seconds for my suitcase on the baggage carousel. I grab it, heading to arrival.

I glance around the crowd where people greeted friends or family as they walk through arrival. Wheeling my suitcase behind me, I search the crowd for my mother's face. I don't see her round face and brunette hair that she always ties in a ponytail. The excitement of seeing my mother for the first time since she and Dad divorced three years ago ran through my veins. At the same time I knew I shouldn't get my hopes up, my heart sinking with disappointment when I don't spot her.

I tell myself not to think she has forgotten to come pick me up, especially when I had spoken to her on Zoom the other day, reminding her about my visit. If she did forget, it wasn't anything new. Ever since she began studying meteorology before she and Dad had broken up, she started to forget everything – special events, Christmas, and birthdays. It was like Dad and I didn't exist in her life anymore or was never a part of it. To her, we were strangers.

Or maybe she went to the wrong airport. I couldn't book a flight until a few days before until Mum knew where she will be on the week I visit. Being a storm chaser, she was on the road a lot between March through June. Kansas City, Missouri was where she said she will be in the area for today. Looking up the weather in advance of what to expect, she said Missouri was the best place for me to meet her there, as storms had been predicted the day before around the area, and it was where she was chasing. What if she had been wrong about the weather, and had chased somewhere else, far from this location?

Before I could worry about Mum forgetting me, I hear her calling out my name as she pushes her way through the crowd. She smiles brightly, waving. I don't return the wave or smile. I couldn't decide whether I should be happy to see her or not. She abandoned me. I didn't even want to come visit her in the first place, but she begged my dad to allow me to come see her. Dad said I had a choice in whether I wanted to see her again. I wasn't going to forgive her at first, but then I decide to give her a second chance. Maybe she has changed.

I stroll over to her, rolling my luggage behind me. She continues to smile, holding her arms out for a hug. I stare at her, debating in my head whether to hug her. Was I making the right decision to be here? I still had a lot of anger towards her for leaving, but at the same time it was great to see her again.

I notice how much she looked different in person than when I chatted to her on Zoom last night. She has aged, looks slimmer and weary with bags under her eyes. No matter how mad I was with her, she was still my mother and I should be thankful to have this chance to reunite with her.

Putting my hatred towards her aside, I let go of my suitcase and embrace her.

"It's good to see you, Mum," I reply. It wasn't a lie. I really was glad to see her, despite what may have happened in the past or how mad I have been with her.

"Oh, Charli, you have no idea how glad I am to hear you say that." She pulls away and strokes my hair. "It's so great to see you, too."

She moves her hands away from my hair and touches my face and then takes my hands, taking in every inch of me before meeting my eyes. "Gosh, you have grown so much."

I let a smile cross my face, unsure if I need to thank her for the compliment.

"How was your trip?" she asks.

"Long and tiring."

Mum laughs. "I know the feeling, sweetie." She grabs my suitcase. "Come on, let's go."

I follow Mum out of the terminal to her car. She leads me towards a black SUV in the far back of the car park. Mum unlocks the vehicle and places my luggage in the boot.

I open the front passenger door and hop in. I eye the video camera on the dashboard as I put on my seat belt. I couldn't understand how Mum could chase storms, not after what happened on our holiday a few years ago.

I turn my eyes away from the camera as Mum climbs into the seat beside me. I don't want to think about my mother's job. I still don't understand why she abandoned Dad and me to pursue a dream she says she had always wanted. To me, why didn't she do it in the first place before marrying Dad if she was just going to leave him later on?

Mum puts on her seat belt. "So tell me what has been happening with you. There is a lot we need to catch up on." She starts the car.

"Where do I start, Mum?" I ask as she pulls out of the parking space. "You *missed* three years of my life."

"Well, you have two weeks of your vacation to tell me all about it." She drives to the exit. "Tell me, do you have a boyfriend?"

I shake my head. For the last remainder of school, my exams were mainly what I tried to focus on the most. When I first learned my parents were getting a divorce, I had accidentally walked in on their conversation. I still picture my Dad's heartbroken face, wondering why Mum had made the decision to leave the both of us. I understand she wanted to pursue her dream, but why wait to do it when your own child is sixteen and needs her mother more than anything? I skipped my school formal even though Dad and my friends encouraged me to attend it. I didn't have the spirit to go. I felt I had the responsibility to help my father get through the divorce. He was a mess once Mum left. There was no time for a boyfriend. There was no room to enjoy the remainder of my teenage life. All I had time for was to make sure Dad didn't go off the rails and fall apart. While I helped him, I often wondered if it was my fault Mum left, and I still think it. I mean, who drops everything to pursue a dream they had always had, like the people around them doesn't matter except for their dream?

"No, I don't have a boyfriend."

She pulls out onto the road. "So how did you do in your HSC?"

"I did well, thanks."

"Are you studying anything?"

I shake my head. I basically put my life on hold after high school. Balancing the remainder of school and making sure Dad was not going to go off the rails, I felt not going on to study was the right thing to do and go straight into the work force to help Dad with bills. That way he wasn't relying on himself keeping food on the table, and a roof over our heads. If Mum had stayed, everything would have been easier. "No. I didn't want to go so I went straight to looking for work. I haven't found anything yet. There is not much work going on right now. Dad helped me save for the trip."

"What kind of work are you looking for?"

"I would like to work in retail, but any job will do. It's very hard to find something when employers ask for experience."

"You will find something soon."

I nod. That's what everyone keeps telling me.

The whole drive to our next destination was me discussing about myself, catching Mum up on everything. I still didn't want to talk about the last three years of my life that Mum missed out on, but I did. Surprisingly she listened and doesn't tell me to stop talking. She never liked me interrupting her or telling her what was going on in my life when she was studying to become a meteorologist. Mum and Dad had a few arguments over her selfish behaviour.

Before I could ask Mum how everything in her life is going, she pulls into a motel parking lot. I look around in confusion, wondering what we were doing here. I knew Mum said she had been out on the road this week, but I didn't think she would be pulling into a motel after picking me up from the airport. I figure she will be making her way to Colorado where she lives.

"What are we doing here, Mum?" I ask her as she parks the car.

She switches off the engine. "I'm just picking up my storm chasing team."

I stare at her, not believing this. Is she seriously thinking of working while I'm visiting? She promised she wouldn't! Mum knew how much I loathed storms after the tornado wiped through our hotel room while we were on holidays. There is no way I wanted to spend my vacation chasing them. Me coming to visit mum meant we would catch up the last three years of our lives, not chase tornadoes.

"Mum, you promised me your job won't interfere with my visit."

Mum takes the keys out of the ignition. "It's not. Charli, sweetie, I'm not doing any storm chasing. My team and I were out storm chasing yesterday, and we spent the night here so I could come pick you up in the morning." She smiles at me. "Come on up to the room. I want you to meet them."

I sigh. Did I really have to meet Mum's team? A team I wanted no part of?

I climb out of the vehicle, and follow Mum upstairs to the second floor. She knocks on room 14. The door opens, revealing a tall man with dark hair standing there. He greets Mum and moves aside for the both of us to enter. There's another guy in the room. He looks to be my age, sitting on the bed, watching something on his video camera. I hear a male's voice in the video, excited about a tornado. My mother's voice follows. The guy looks up for a second at Mum and I as we entered before turning back to the video.

"Tommy, this is my daughter, Charli," Mum introduces me to the man who had answered the door. "Charli, this is my storm chasing partner, Tommy."

A smile spreads across Tommy's face as he holds out his hand for me to shake. "It's a pleasure to meet you."

I stare at his large hand before shaking it, giving him a half smile.

"And this is Blake," Mum continues on, turning to the guy sitting on the bed. He pauses the video and looks up at us. His dark brown eyes meet mine. "Blake is Tommy's friend's son, who is doing an internship with us. He is eighteen like you, so I'm sure you two will get along really well."

Blake gives me a small smile. I return it. He then goes back to his video.

"April, are you sure you don't want to storm chase today?" Tommy asks, sitting down on the bed across from Blake, picking up his laptop. "The radar is showing a lot of storm activity around Oklahoma. I reckon if we leave now, we could possibly see a tornado by the afternoon before it gets dark."

My stomach twist into knots, knowing straight away my mother wasn't going to keep her promise over Tommy's offer. The thought of all the storm activity Tommy spoke about made my head spin.

Mum sighs with disappointment. "Tommy, my daughter is here. I promised her I wasn't going to do any chasing while she visits."

Tommy looks my way, and I see the accusation of my present in his eyes, interfering with their work by being here. He turns his gaze back to Mum. "Are you sure, April? The activity around Oklahoma looks big."

"Even if we go ahead with this chase, Oklahoma is five hours away. Do you think we would have enough time to get down there?"

"Yes, I do. It's almost ten, and we need to check out of this room in the next few minutes. We will leave soon and head down there. This storm may hit by late afternoon."

Mum joins Tommy at his side. She glances over his shoulder, placing her hand on her chin as she stares at the radar on Tommy's laptop, thinking hard. Blake puts down his camera, and stands at Mum's side to catch a glimpse of the storm. I lean against the TV stand, hoping I don't have to stay here any longer, or have to be grabbed into a storm chase I want no part of. I watch Mum carefully as she thinks, and I could sense she was going to give in to her partner's request. I didn't even have to ask Mum what she was thinking. I could feel her thoughts, knowing she was going to go along with this chase even if I am here. She worshipped storms. As long as I could remember before she decided she wanted to live her passion, she was always outside watching a developing storm. She encouraged me to share her passion, but storms were something I never enjoyed, even before the tornado. There was no way she was going to miss out on this opportunity.

Definitely not for me anyway.

Mum nods. "You're right. This storm cell looks huge. It may even produce multiple tornadoes."

"What do you say?" Tommy's eyes never leaving the radar. "Should we chase this storm? Or do you want to leave it so you can spend some time with your daughter?" He may not have looked my way when he says this, but the annoyance in his voice of my present is clear as day. I already have the feeling Tommy and I weren't going to get along well. Tommy probably will not forgive me if Mum doesn't take the request with the following this storm, like it was the only thing that mattered. "We could collect incredible data for this storm."

A smile spreads across Mum's face, nodding as she turns to Tommy. "You're right. This storm is too good to miss out on data." She turns to me, giving me an apologetic smile. "What do you say, Charli? Do you want to do some storm chasing? It will be an amazing experience."

I frown. Did Mum really think that this will be an amazing experience? From what I have seen in video footage of these storms is devastating. Doesn't she remember the last time we had an encounter with a tornado? I couldn't see this as an amazing experience. I saw it as suicidal. *This* is not what I came here for. I came here to spend time with my mother, not chase after tornadoes and put my own life at risk. I don't care if it's part of Mum's job. Dad would *never* allow Mum to put me in this kind of danger.

Without answering my mother, I leave the room.

Chapter 2

Mum calls out to me, but her call only makes me walk swiftly towards her car. I go to open the boot, but of course it's lock. I let out a small frustrating scream as I slam my palm against the door.

Mum stands beside me, reaching out. I move out of the way before she could lay a finger on me.

"Keep away from me, Mum," I warn her. "I don't want to speak or see you again."

I see the hurt in her eyes from my words. "Charli, please. Don't say those things."

I threw my arms in the air, not giving a damn with how rude I was to my mother. "Why? You don't really care about me. You left me, Mum. You left me so you can come here to pursue your dream as a storm chaser. And when you asked Dad if it was okay I come visit you, you were excited about it. You said you wanted to catch up and spend some time with me. At first I wasn't really sure if I should have come here, but Dad said to give you another chance. You said you won't do any storm chasing while we are here."

Mum nods. "I know, Charli, and you are right. Listen, let me do this one job today, and I promise you that tomorrow we will do something together. We will catch up on everything."

12

"According to the forecast for this week there will be a lot of supercells developing with possible tornadoes," Tommy says from behind Mum. "You did say the other day that you wanted to catch every single one of them, April."

I look past my mother's shoulder to see Tommy and Blake heading over to us. I roll my eyes, shaking my head as I let out a frustrating sigh. If they weren't here, my mum wouldn't be making this decision to go on a chase. We would be driving to her home and starting our two week vacation together if it wasn't for them.

Mum turns around to face him. "I know what I said, Tommy. But that was before I remembered Charli was coming to visit."

My heart sinks in my chest. Mum had forgotten I was coming to visit. She probably never even wanted me to come here in the first place, only wanting to see me to make it seem like she was still interested when really she wasn't. If I hadn't contacted her the other day to remind her, I would have been left stranded at the airport. The trip my Dad had paid for me would have been a total waste of time then.

And maybe this trip is a waste of time. I should never have agreed to come.

"You forgot about me?" I choke on my words. "After you suggested I come out here to visit you?"

Mum shakes her head. "No, Charli. I never forgot about you."

"Cut the bull crap, Mum. You did forget about me. Just like you had forgotten mine and Dad's birthday for the past few years, and fail to contact us on Christmas, as well as other celebrations. You act like we don't exist."

"Charli, I'm sorry. Work has been really crazy."

"I don't care about your job or how crazy it is. I want you to take notice of me for a change."

I turn to see if I could open the boot again, but it's still lock. I pound my palm on the window. Why the hell does this vacation have to start off like this? I demand for the car to be unlock. Mum listens, unlocking it with her remote control. As soon as I hear the click, I open the boot and grab my luggage.

"Where are you going, Charli?" she asks as I slam the boot shut.

I began walking towards the street, my luggage wheeling behind me. "I'm going back to the airport. This trip is a total waste of time."

Mum calls me back, but I have already made up my mind. I am going home. It's all for the best. Tommy tells me to let me go. Yes, Mum. Let me go. You don't want me here so why beg me to stay?

I don't dare to look back at Mum once I reach the street. I turn right, following the road Mum had come down earlier. I didn't get very far when I hear footsteps running on the pavement behind me. I roll my eyes. Why is Mum bothering to chase after me? Doesn't she understand when I said I don't want to see her ever again?

I sigh. "Mum, just leave me alone."

"You shouldn't talk to your mother like that."

I stop and turn around to see Blake following me with his video camera still in his hand. I frown at the sight of him. Mum must have sent him after me.

"Don't tell me how I should treat my mother," I snap at him. "You don't know anything about her."

"Actually, I do. I have been working with her since tornado season started this year. She is a really nice and dedicated woman."

14

I bite my lip, fighting back the tears that threatened to fall. He was right. Mum had always been nice. She was easily approachable by many people, always willing to help out whenever she could. She was dedicated, putting all of her efforts into something she really cared about. She used to be a nurse, always dedicated to spend most of her time at the hospital, helping ill people. Even when she had her day off, Mum spent it with Dad and me rather than spending the day on herself. But ever since the disaster had led her to want to study meteorology and follow her passion of studying storms, she had changed. She was still dedicated, but she didn't seem like the mother I had once known. She was still nice and friendly to others, but would often snap at Dad and me if we ever got in the way of her studying, becoming selfish towards us.

Then again, my whole family changed that day after it almost claimed our lives.

When she first announced she was going to do an internship in America to study meteorology, she didn't ask if Dad and I wanted to go. She said it will only be for three months. I try to contact her while she was over there to see how she was and to let her know what was going on in my life. I video chatted with her whenever I could, but with the time difference it was hard, and when I do manage to get a hold of her, she didn't have the time to talk because she had to work. A few days after she returned home, she decided she wanted to move to the US to study more about tornadoes. This time she asked if we wanted to go, but we both said no. I had my friends here who I didn't want to leave behind, and of course Dad had his job as well. The idea of living in Tornado Alley terrified me, and I couldn't understand why Mum wanted to place herself in danger there or even put her family's lives at risk. I beg Mum not to go, but she went anyway. I waited for tornado season to be over, hoping she would return home safely, but she didn't. Dad and I wait for a call from her to let us know when she was returning home, but she never contacted us, never even bothered to wish me a happy birthday in August. My worse fear was she had been killed in a chase. In mid-October she finally returned home, asking my dad if she could file for divorce.

I loathed my mother for the decisions she had made. She had left me. She had left Dad. She didn't need to, but she did. When I think about it now, the divorce was all for the best. At least I know Dad would never abandon me to pursue his dreams. And if he did, he would have made sure I agreed with him first before he made a final decision.

"If she is so nice, why did she abandon me?" It's the one question I ask myself over and over again. I have never been able to answer it at all. "Did she ever mention that to you?"

Blake stares at me blankly, processing my words. I wait for him to say something, whether if it was to defend my mother or if he agreed with me.

When he doesn't respond, I continue my way down the path.

"She talks about you," Blake calls out. "She does love you even if she might not show it."

I stop, turning back to him.

"Look, I know it's not right for what she has done," he continues, "but from the little time I have spent with her, she is a really nice person. And despite what she has done, you should never say horrible things about your mother."

"Whatever."

I resume walking.

"You do realise how far the airport is from here," Blake calls out.

"And why would you care about how far I have to walk?" I say without stopping, or turning to look back at him.

"Well, for one thing you will be soaked once you get there if it does rain, unless you have an umbrella somewhere in your luggage."

I stop to stare up at the sky. The clouds were a dark grey, looking as if it might rain at any moment. He was right. If I walk, I would be soaked. But maybe I don't have to walk. I could find a bus that heads in the direction.

"Besides, I wouldn't be walking if I was you," he continues.

"That's because you aren't me."

"True, I'm not. But just so you know, tornadoes are very unpredictable. Even if our weather radar shows where all of the possible ones are going to be, it doesn't mean it will happen. Sometimes the weather patterns can change or it might not show up on the radar, and because it looks like it might rain, you never know when one might appear. Sometimes we end up chasing the wrong storm cell that will only give us a thunderstorm and no tornado."

I glance up at the sky. I knew nothing about tornadoes, but I knew the damage they can do within seconds. I had studied natural disasters in Geography, but when it came to storms, I didn't want to know anything about them.

Before I could say anything else, Tommy pulls up beside us at the wheel. Mum sits beside him.

"Come on you, two," she says. "We really need to get onto the road if we want to catch this storm."

Blake opens the back door and climbs in, while I stand there on the sidewalk.

"Come on, Charli," Mum says. "Get in the car."

I shake my head. "No. I'm not coming with you. I'm not going anywhere near those storms. Don't you remember what happened when we went on holidays last time? Right before you decided to study meteorology?"

Mum stares at me, like she is thinking but doesn't know how to respond to my question. She remembers. I know she does. She knows how badly effected I was after the disaster happened. My phobia for storms developed that day, never wanting to be in anything like that again. But it wasn't like Mum paid attention to how I really felt. It was about what she wanted. And when she turns her eyes away from me, looking straight ahead, I knew nothing has changed about her attitude towards my phobia.

"What happened before you studied meteorology?" Tommy asks Mum.

She shakes her head. "It's nothing. It's not important right now."

My stomach twists into knots. What happened that day when I was only thirteen, the day that could have claimed my family's life, Mum thought it wasn't important to discuss. It was something my parents and I never discuss. It was a day we much rather forget, but we all knew deep down inside we couldn't and never will.

Turning away before anyone could see the tears forming in my eyes, I walk away. I ignore Mum's plead for me to get in the car. I didn't get very far when my luggage is snatch from my hand.

I spin around to see Blake carrying my luggage towards the car.

Wiping my eyes, I stroll after him, demanding he hands my suitcase over. He ignores my request, and places it in the boot. He then turns to me, picking me off the ground and throwing me over his shoulder. I scream, demanding to be let go, slapping him hard on his back. Blake sits me down in the back seat, squeezing himself in the seat beside me so I couldn't jump out.

As soon as Blake closes the door, Tommy pulls away from the kerb. Blake puts on his seat belt. I sat there, refusing to put mine on. Why should I when I didn't ask to be in this car?

Mum glances over her shoulder at me. "Sweetie, you need to put on your seat belt."

"No. Let me out of this car."

"Charli, listen to me. We are going to chase this tornado. I promise you after we chase this storm, I will be done with work. Then it will just be you and me."

I stare at Mum, unsure if I wanted to believe her lies. Maybe she is telling the truth this time, but then again she promises everything, breaking them later. Beside me I could feel Blake's eyes on me, and it irritated me as everyone waited for my response.

I sigh; giving in to my mother's constant nagging. "Fine. I will go. But only for this chase and that's it."

Chapter 3

I pull out my phone, blasting music through my ears, staring out of the window at towns, cities and farm lands. The music helps me to relax a bit, putting aside all the things that happened earlier. There is not much chatter in the car, except for Tommy and Mum discussing which roads to take or talking about what's new on the radar. Blake sits beside me, viewing something on his phone.

Mum doesn't speak to me during the whole car ride, focusing everything on her job. I'm thankful she doesn't acknowledge me. I'm not in the mood to talk to her.

As we enter Oklahoma, Tommy pulls the SUV into a service station to fill up.

Mum unbuckles her seat belt and then turns towards me. "Charli, would you like anything to eat?"

I don't respond, even when my stomach grumbles from the mention of food.

Mum sighs. "Honey, you can ignore me all you want, but eventually you will have to talk to me."

I stare out the window so I don't have to look at my mother. When she realises she wasn't getting a response from me, she gets out of the car, heading towards the service station.

As soon as Mum is gone, Blake speaks next. "If you need to use the bathroom, you better do so now because once we start chasing, you won't be able to. And if you are hungry, you better grab something now. We won't be stopping again."

Without saying anything else, Blake gets out of the car. I sit there for a moment, wondering if I too should get out. Stretching my legs would be good, especially when we have been driving for so long.

I make a decision, getting out of the car just as two vehicles with radars and satellite stuff on their roof pulls in. Great. More storm chasers. The men get out and greet Tommy, discussing the weather.

I glance up at the clouds. They were light grey where we were, but to the south they were a darker shade, almost a midnight blue.

I head inside the store, walking down the aisles, unsure what I wanted to eat. I settle on something healthy, unlike the junk I see Blake picking up – potato chips, lollies, chocolate and soft drink. I pick up a ham and cheese sandwich and a bottle of water. I notice Blake watching me, but doesn't say anything and heads straight towards the counter to pay for his items. I stand behind him as Mum moves away from the counter after paying for the petrol. She heads back outside.

Blake moves forward and places his items on the counter. The clerk scans them, placing everything into a paper bag. He pays for it and then steps aside for me. He waits for me to pay for my things, and then walks me back to the car.

"You really should start speaking to the rest of us," he tells me. "I get it you're mad at your mother, but it doesn't mean you can just give us *all* the silent treatment."

I keep my eyes ahead instead of responding.

Mum and Tommy stood in front of the bonnet of the SUV, glancing at the laptop that sat there.

"I reckon this is going to hit Fullerton," Mum says.

"Are you sure?" Tommy asks. "It looks like it might be on the outskirts of Fullerton and Woodville to the east."

"We could head in that direction. Once we reach Fullerton, we will be able to figure out which position we should set ourselves in."

Tommy looks up at Blake and me as we join them. "What do you think, Blake?"

Blake shrugs. "I'm up for whatever you think is right."

"Right, let's get going, shall we? I want this to be a non-stop trip to Fullerton."

We hop into the SUV, heading towards the town of Fullerton. We munch on our snacks, deciding where to go. I had my earphones in, barely hearing anything on the conversation about the storm.

It takes us another twenty minutes to get to the town. By then the clouds are so dark that it looked like dusk, almost night. Flashes of lightning rips through the sky, follow by thunder clapping. Even with the volume up high on my phone, it doesn't fully block out the sound of thunder.

I glance around at everyone as they showed fascination towards the developing storm. I sit there, trying to keep calm as my breathing speeds up and so does my heart rate. I bite my lip as hard as I could to prevent me from screaming, and then try to hide my face so no one could see the tears in my eyes.

I need to get out of this car. I need to hide. I don't care where I hide. Just somewhere so I will feel safe during the storm.

Tommy turns off the main road, moving away from the town into farm land. He pulls over onto the kerb, jumping out of the car as soon as he applies the brake. Blake jumps out after him. Mum turns to me while I sit there frozen with fear.

"Honey, do you want to come out and check out the sky?" she asks me.

I shake my head, refusing to look at her. I don't want her to see the tears in my eyes.

Mum stares at me for a moment, hoping I would change my mind. When I don't respond to her, she gets out of the vehicle. Once I was alone, I unbuckle my seat belt, lying down on the backseat, curling into a ball. I let the tears flow down my cheeks as the thunder rumbles loudly. The music doesn't calm me anymore. The thunder is too loud for the music to drown it out, and I could not put the volume up any higher without damaging my ear drums. I take out my ear phones and place them in my pocket, along with my phone. I cover my ears, wanting this all to end. Outside I can hear the others talking excitedly over the developing storm. Mum and Tommy discuss where the best position will be to observe the clouds and where a wall cloud might form. Blake spots a wall cloud to the east over near a hill. How were they all excited over this? How could anyone be excited in hoping a tornado would form out of a supercell?

Something thumps hard on the roof of the SUV.

"Hail!" Blake screams. "We have got hail!"

The hail belted down. Still curled up in a ball, I mumble to myself as I squeeze my eyes shut for all of this to be over.

Blake opens the door on the driver's side. "Are you alright, Charli?"

"Charli, what's wrong?" Mum asks as she climbs into the front seat.

I don't respond to neither of them as I continue to mumble to myself.

"April, we need to get going," Tommy says, closing his door.

"Blake, sit in the front," Mum orders.

I don't open my eyes to see what's happening. All I hear is hail continuing to belt down, and thunder clapping loudly, Mum's and Blake's footsteps crushing the gravel, Blake cursing as a hail stone hits him. I hear a door slam. I then feel a pair of hands lifting me up into a sitting position. Mum slams the door and tells Tommy to go.

Tommy pulls away from the kerb as Mum pulls me into her arms. I wanted to pull away, knowing this was probably an act and she didn't really care how I feel. But right now, I didn't care about our broken relationship. The feeling of her arms around me comforts me. It made me remember when she used to cuddle up to me when I was younger whenever I felt unwell, scared or injured. Sometimes she would comfort me during storms, but most of the time Dad was the one to comfort me. When a storm happened and I was at home, I'd always hide until it was over. Sometimes Dad will join me in my hiding place and cradle me in his arms. If I was home alone or at a friend's place, I hid under the covers of my bed until it was safe to come out. If I was driving and a storm approaches, I have to pull over, hiding in the backseat until it passes. When Dad drives, he has to pull over for me until the storm passes.

Mum strokes my hair. "It's okay, baby. It's okay."

Mum's smoothing words help me to calm down. I open my eyes as soon the hail stops belting down. The sound of the hail is replaced by the rain as it patters down on the roof.

Blake turns around to face us. I quickly wipe the tears from my eyes, not wanting to know what he thinks or how I might look after crying. He probably thinks I am overreacting, especially with how tough I acted earlier.

"How is she, April?" Tommy asks.

"Charli is fine," Mum replies.

No, I'm not fine! I wanted to say, but I couldn't speak through the terror.

Blake turns to look at Mum's laptop that is sitting on his lap. It showed the weather radar of our current location. Every morning before I left the house, I always checked the weather and read the radars so I could prepare myself when a storm does come. I couldn't read it properly where I was sitting but I knew no doubt this storm wasn't going to be good.

He clicks something on the screen and a video pops up beside the radar of a weather report. "Hey, the National Weather Service just issued a tornado warning."

I hear the excitement in my mother's voice as she says, "Excellent."

I scream silently in my head. Can't all of this be over already?

When we reach the hill, Tommy pulls over and gets out of the car, with Blake following straight behind him. Tommy calls out that there is rotation in the northeast.

Mum turns to me. "Come on, sweetie. Come out and have a look."

I shake my head. "No, I can't."

Mum strokes my face. "Charli, I know you are terrified. But you should come out and take a look."

"No."

"Come on, Charli."

"Mum, I said no. I have been in a tornado, and I do not *ever* want to see another one again."

"I get it, Charli. You're terrified of storms. Listen, do you know the best way to face your fear?"

"Mum, Dad has tried to get me to take programs to help me face my fear. It never helped."

"Funnel!" Blake screams. "We have a funnel!"

Mum smiles at me. "I know how to help you face your fear."

There's an uneasy feeling in my stomach, knowing I won't like whatever Mum says next. "I don't want to know what will help."

She takes my hand. "I was scared too, Charli, when we were in that tornado. Studying these storms have helped me to overcome the fear. It has helped me to see the beauty of a storm."

"I'm not you, Mum. And what do you mean there is a beauty side of the storm? I don't see the beauty of them."

Mum doesn't answer my question. There was no convincing her how getting out in the storm to observe the developing tornado was a bad idea. "Come on. Come out here and have a look."

To avoid another argument, I allowed my mother to lead me out of the car and stand on the side of the road where Tommy and Blake were. Blake films the developing tornado.

The rain pats down, instantly drenching my clothes, making it stick to my skin. The wind picks up. While the others all watched the clouds in awe, I was the only one breathing heavily, ready for another panic attack, planning an escape plan silently in my head.

I glance around me, jumping every time lightning flashes through the sky or when thunder clap loudly. The vortex was almost to the ground. Tommy spots another funnel forming near the road beside us.

"We need to move a little further up the road," Tommy suggests. "When it lands, it may head our way."

Mum agrees and then runs to the back of the car, pulling something out of the boot. Tommy helps her move an orange cone to the side of the road. I have no idea what it was, maybe something to collect data with. Blake closes the back boot.

The others climb back into the car, while I stand there, eyeing the funnels. I need to find shelter, but where could I hide out here in the open once the tornadoes do touch ground? I can hide in the car, but hiding there wasn't a smart idea during a tornado.

Panicking, I turn on my heel in the direction we have driven down, running away from the car. Mum yells at me to get in the car, but I ignore her as my anxiety completely takes over me. I can't think. I run down the road as fast I could. I know I should be getting in the car, but the vehicle didn't make me feel safe. Nowhere did. Being out in the open didn't make me feel like I was out of harm's way. My mind kept telling me that there was no safe place to be. Just being on this chase didn't make feel like I was out of danger.

"It's on the ground!" Tommy yells. "The tornado is on the ground!"

Chapter 4

I stop at the sound of Tommy's voice, and turn around to see the funnel cloud we had been observing from the northeast had touched down. The winds are even stronger now than before it had reached the ground, whistling loudly. My hair blows all over the place, even when it was tied into a ponytail, the rain making it stick to my face. Leaves and tree branches blew in my direction as the tornado snapped the trees near the road. I had to quickly dodge out of the way so I couldn't be hit by debris. The strong winds made it impossible to stand. The vortex moves east, moving away from me.

Blake runs towards me. Mum goes to follow him, but then stops, looking to the right. She curses.

"Blake, Charli, take shelter now!" she screams over the loud whopping, as she runs back to Tommy who yells at her to get into the car.

Blake continues to run, telling me to duck down in a ditch beside the road, pointing to my right. I look in the direction he was pointing. The second funnel was also on the ground, heading in my direction, the wind whistling loudly. It was getting harder to stand still without the wind trying to sweep me off the ground. I should be running, but I was frozen on the spot, my mind yelling at me to take shelter, but my body refused to move. I couldn't think, not with the thunder echoing through the sky and the roaring winds of the tornado.

I hear the tyres of Tommy's car screeching on the tar road to move quickly away from the tornado. Blake struggles to run as he heads towards me. When he reaches me, he grabs my arm, pulling me to the side of the road, pushing me into a ditch. He puts an arm around me, telling me to stay low and to cover my head. I listen to him, even though it was hard to hear through the roaring winds.

Within seconds the twister was near us. I scream as the wind tugs on me, threatening to pull both Blake and me into the air. Dirt, leaves, grass, and branches that the other tornado had blown in our direction, flew around us. I was thankful there was nothing too big, such as houses, nearby for the tornado to drop on top of us.

Luckily for us, the whirling vortex narrowly passes us on our left, heading into the direction of the other tornado. Blake and I lie there for a second until the winds subsided. I could still hear the roaring winds in the distance. Even when the tornado has passed, I still scream from the terror of what had happened, and the thunder clapping in the sky didn't help at all.

My body trembles as Blake helps me off the ground. He pulls me into his arms, letting me cry into his chest as he calms me down. When I'm calm, he pulls away from me.

"What the hell were you thinking?" Blake asks, frowning. "Are you trying to get yourself killed?"

My mouth trembles as tears flow down my cheeks. "I'm sorry. I-I don't know what came over me. I-I panicked."

"Yes, you did panic. And you endangered your life, as well as mine for pulling that dangerous stunt. Don't you know anything about tornadoes?"

I bite my lip to stop myself from saying something nasty that will lead to an argument. Right now I didn't feel like fighting at all. I wanted to get out of this rain and out of these wet clothes, find somewhere safe out of this storm.

I glance at the ground, refusing to make eye contact with Blake as his words stab me in the stomach. Seeing the anger in his eyes made me feel like a complete fool. I don't know what came over me when I ran out into the path of a tornado rather than seeking shelter in the car. Sometimes I don't think at all when I have a panic attack during a storm.

Tommy pulls up next to us. Mum jumps out and runs over to me, wrapping her arms around me, while Tommy checks on Blake, who says he is alright.

"What were you thinking, Charli?" Mum asks me, pulling away as she rests her hands on my arms.

I couldn't look at her either. I didn't want to see the tears forming in her eyes. Whether or not if they were real tears or fake ones to make me believe she cared, I didn't want her to worry about me. She never worried about me before. Not until I decided to do something stupid to endanger my own life.

When I don't answer her, she pats my hair, pushing back the wet strands from my face, giving me a smile.

"Thank goodness you are alright, Charli," she says.

That's when I force myself to look at her. Mom's eyes were fill with hurt, fear and worry. I knew then as much as I didn't want to believe she cared; she actually did. Despite her abandoning Dad and me to chase her dreams, ignoring us like we were strangers to her, deep down inside I still meant a lot to her.

Mum pulls me into another hug, tighter than before. Over her shoulder I catch a glimpse of Blake, who watches me carefully. He shows no emotion, and I wasn't sure if he was still angry with me or if there was another emotion he felt towards me after the stunt I had pulled. Maybe he felt bad for the words he had said earlier before Mum and Tommy pulled up beside us to make sure we were alright, and didn't want to hold a grudge at me for too long.

Tommy glances up at the sky before turning towards the twisters as they disappear into the distance, heading towards a property I can just see being destroyed. Tree branches were scattered all over the road.

"We should get going and follow the storm," he says, turning back to us. "It looks like it's heading towards the town of Woodville. We should head in that direction to see if anyone needs help."

I scream inside my head. How can he want to follow the storm after what has happened to Blake and I?

Mum nods, pulling away. "Right. First let's get the cone. Do you know if the tornado passed over it?"

Tommy shrugs. "I don't think it did. I didn't see anything when we sped away."

"We will check the data later when we find a motel for the night."

Mum and Tommy walks over to the orange cone still on the side of the road, barely moved from its spot when the tornado came by. I stand there as I watch Blake climb into the backseat of the SUV. I don't move until once Mum and Tommy get the cone in the back of the SUV, and then tell me to get in. I sit in the backseat, refusing to make eye contact with Blake. I didn't even want to glance out of the window at the devastation the tornadoes have caused. Even though I stared at the back of Tommy's seat in front of me, I could see the debris from the corner of my eye.

Tommy drives slowly down the road, being careful of the debris. One car coming from the opposite direction to us was parked on the side of the road, where a tree with the roots still intact was lying in front of it, just inches away from the vehicle. Tommy rolls down his window and pulls up alongside them where a lady and man, Spanish descent, were in the front seat.

"Are you two alright?" Tommy asks.

The man sitting in the driver's seat answers yes. "The tree just narrowly missed us, and we managed to get out of the way from the path of the tornado."

"No one is hurt?"

"No."

Tommy resumes down the road, both him and my mother abandoning the chase, now just examining the destruction. The tornadoes were far ahead of us, and it was pointless continuing the chase. Tommy and Mum check on passing motorist or anyone on nearby properties if they were alright. Since we weren't on a busy road, there weren't any flipped cars or trucks at all; only people who managed to dodge out of the way before they were sucked up into the air by the winds, avoiding any debris thrown their way.

Tommy pulls into a gravel driveway, leading up to the property I saw the tornado destroy in the distance. A barn was completely done, while the farm house had only the interior left standing.

Everyone gets out of the vehicle while I take my time getting out, unsure if I wanted to see the devastation the tornadoes had caused.

I look around at the debris where a car had been tossed into the building, and broken trees scattered amongst the rubble. A tree Tommy had parked near was still standing with no leaves and was debarked.

Tommy and Mum scream out to anyone who could have been trapped underneath the rubble, while Blake helped search as he filmed everything. I glance around, feeling helpless, memories flooding back to me of the time the tornado struck the hotel we had stayed at while on holidays. It's a day I much rather forget. I don't understand how Mum left Dad and me for this job. How could she handle this every tornado season?

A storm shelter door opens near the damage building. Mum and Tommy hurries over to them to check if the family of four was alright. They answered fine, saying they got into the shelter in time.

While they talk, I hop back into the car, closing my eyes as I rest my head against the door, taking deep breathes. I listen to the thunder that was now subsiding as the storm moves away.

"Are you alright?" I hear Blake ask me.

I open my eyes to see him standing beside the door. I don't answer him straight away. "How can you do this job?"

Blake shrugs. "I just come to film, while Tommy and April collects data."

I shake my head, wiping the tears from my eyes. I hope Mum doesn't continue to bring me along with her on these chases. I couldn't handle being out here. Chasing tornadoes was not what I had in mind when wanting to catch up with her.

She and Tommy soon return to the car. Within minutes we were back on the road, driving by the destructive path the tornadoes have travelled through. I couldn't bring myself to glance out of the window as we drive into the town of Woodville, where many buildings were nothing but rubble, while other buildings were completely untouched or some had minor damage.

Tommy, Mum and Blake got out of the car to help out the best they could. I remain inside the vehicle, curling up into a ball in the backseat, crying as the memories of the day that I could have loss my family or my own life flooded into my mind.

Chapter 5

I enter the motel room Mum and I was sharing, and headed straight to the bathroom to take a shower. I stay in there for at least half an hour as I wash off the dirt from when Blake and I were in the ditch. When I come out, I find Mum sitting on the double bed, her laptop opened in front of her. The television is also on, broadcasting about the tornadoes that hit the outskirts of Fullerton and the town of Woodville, most likely an EF3.

Mum looks up at me when she sees me standing there in my pyjamas. She smiles at me. "Hey, how was the shower?"

"Good."

She pats the bed beside her, gesturing for me to sit beside her. I listen to her. Mum studies the radar on her screen for tomorrow, and other graphs that I didn't quite understand what they were. My stomach twists into knots, knowing straight away she wasn't going to keep her word. I wonder if I should remind her how I really didn't want to do anymore storm chasing, even if she has to work.

"How are you after today?" Mum asks me.

"The same way I felt when we went on holidays and that tornado hit."

Mum put her laptop down for a moment and puts an arm around me, pulling me close to her. "I thought you would be over your fear by now."

"I never got over it."

Mum plays with the wet strands of my hair. "I'm sorry about everything earlier."

"It's fine. Don't worry about it." I stare at the radar. "That orange cone you put on the road, what was that?"

"It's something Tommy and I put together to help with research. It has built in cameras which captures the tornado from every angle, and collects data to help us learn more about them. It measures the wind speed when it crosses over it. We also designed it so it wouldn't be picked up by the winds. So far we haven't been successful for this season. We haven't been able to put it in the direct path of the vortex. Tornadoes are so unpredictable that you never know which way they will go or where they will land. Next year Tommy and I want to invest a vehicle that will allow us to get closer without being picked up by the winds."

I nod slowly, pretending to take an interest in her work.

A knock comes from the door. Mum didn't have to ask who it was, and calls out to Tommy to enter the room.

"Hey." Tommy closes the door and crosses the room over to us.

Mum smiles at him. "Hey." She turns to me. "Charli, do you mind giving us a second?"

I nod, grabbing my phone on the bedside table and head outside. Once I closed the door behind me, Mum and Tommy wait for a second before they begin talking. I press my ear against the door to hear.

"Do you think she is going to be able to handle another chase?" Tommy asks.

"I'm not sure, Tommy."

"If she is going to act like this, we can't bring her on the chase. She won't only be endangered to herself, but to all of us."

"I know, I know. It's just that Charli has this phobia about storms. She had it since we went on this holiday six years ago. There was this cyclone up north that produced multiple tornadoes down south. We were in the path of one of them. I thought Charli was over the fear, but it's clear she isn't. Besides, I don't know if I should go on another chase. I promised her I would spend time with her. It's why I invited her to come visit in the first place."

"April, the season is almost over. We still need to collect data. And you did tell me that you wanted to chase as many tornadoes as we can during the season. Plus, Blake still needs to shoot more footage for his video. You made these promises before Charli arrived here. You didn't even tell me about her visiting until two days ago."

"I know, I did, Tommy. I will explain to her in the morning that I need to work. If we do get a free day off from chasing, then we will do something together."

I move away from the door, not wanting to hear any more of the conversation. Not if it was going to make me angry. I couldn't get into an argument with Mum here at the motel where everyone could hear.

I pull out my phone and call my dad, anything to distract me from Mum. I had promised him I would call once I landed, but after everything that happened this afternoon, I had forgotten to call him. I have no idea what time it was back at home, but whatever the time is, I'm sure Dad wouldn't mind if I call too late or too early.

"Hey, sweetie, how's it going?" Dad's cheery voice greets me when he picks up.

I smile into the receiver, wishing he could see it. "Hey, Dad. I hope I haven't caught you in a bad time."

"Nope, you haven't. I'm at work at the moment. It's not too busy at the office, so I'm able to talk. So how's it going? What have you been up to?"

I nod slowly, biting my lip so I couldn't cry. I couldn't tell him about today. I don't want him to worry about my safety. And if I tell him how Mum wasn't taking much interest in me besides her job, he wouldn't be happy with her. He would demand to speak to her, and I didn't want Mum to feel I've told on her.

"I'm great, Dad. Mum and I haven't really done much yet. We mostly talked and caught up with things."

I feel Dad's smile on the other end. If only he knew the truth, he wouldn't be smiling. "That's great to know. Have you two made any plans yet?"

I shrug. "No, I don't know what we are doing yet. We will make plans in the morning."

And unfortunately, I don't get much say in what I want, because it's most likely I will have to go storm chasing whether I liked it or not.

"Listen, I better get back to work," he says. "We can catch up later and you can tell me all about the fun you're having."

"Okay," I say softly, disappointed that I couldn't speak to him longer.

I hang up and then stand there for a moment, feeling bad for lying to Dad about my trip. Still holding onto my phone, I glance up at the sky. The clouds have cleared and the stars shine brightly in the night sky. A cool breeze blows, making me shiver briefly.

"Is everything alright?" I hear Blake's voice.

I jump at the sound of his voice, swirling around to see him sitting on the ground, leaning up against the wall next to the entry of the door to the room he and Tommy shared, with his laptop in front of him. I didn't even know he was sitting there.

"How long have you been sitting there for?" I ask.

"Since Tommy walked into your room. I came to sit out here because it felt stuffy in our room."

"So you were listening in on my phone call?"

He raises his eyebrow. "Not on purpose. You should speak for yourself. You listened in on your mother's and Tommy's conversation. So don't accuse me of eavesdropping when you did the exact same thing."

He had a point, and I knew I couldn't get upset with him.

"I don't think Tommy likes me very much," I say, crossing my arms across my chest.

"Why do you say that?"

I shrug. "I don't know. I guess because I'm getting in the way of the chase, and doesn't like me visiting my mum. Hey, do you mind if I join you?"

Blake nods. "Yeah, sure." He turns to his computer screen.

I sit down beside him, leaning my back up against the door and cross my legs. I glance over at his computer screen where he was on an editing program, playing around with clips of tornadoes he had filmed.

"What are you doing?" I ask him.

"I'm putting together a film about tornadoes," he answers without taking his eyes away from the screen. "It's a class project I have to put together over the summer break. I had no idea what I was going to do my project on, so Tommy asked if I wanted to do an internship. Not only do I get to film things for my video, but I also get to film things for the weather channel. Some of my footage has even been sold to the news channels."

"So you're going to become like a director or something?"

He looks up at me and nods. "Yeah, I hope to someday."

He turns back to the screen. I watch him cut scenes, playback videos and figuring out which clips should go where.

I thought about today, and wondered whether if he disliked me after what I did earlier today.

"Listen, I want to apologise again for what happened this afternoon," I say.

He looks up at me. "You don't need to keep apologising."

"I know. I just... I feel really stupid and I don't want you to hate me for putting your life at risk."

Blake stares at me for a long time before closing his laptop. "I don't hate you for what you did, Charli. I'm just angry for what you did. It's beyond stupidity for the stunt you pulled. I understand you panicked, but I don't understand why you would put yourself in danger like that."

I bite my lip. "I know."

"What happened out there today? Not just with you running out into the path of a tornado, but when you were crying in the car."

"I have astraphobia."

"That's a fear of thunder and lightning, right?"

I nod. "Yeah."

"How long have you had the fear?"

"I had it since I was thirteen."

"What brought on the fear?"

I look away from him for a moment, reliving the day in my mind. I try not to think about it, but it's not something you can just forget overnight.

"My parents and I were on holidays on the Gold Coast in Australia. Up north there was a cyclone, and it travelled down south. Even though we were miles away from the cyclone, it sent all of this rain our way, completely ruining our holiday. Some places had flash flooding while other places were struck by tornadoes. It was stormy when we went out to lunch, and when we were just returning to the hotel, that's when the tornado came without warning. I was thirteen, and I felt confused when I saw the tornado for the first time. It's rare to see them in Australia, unlike what it is in the United States, I wasn't sure what was going on. All I remember is my dad grabbing my hand and my mother's, pulling us inside for shelter. Since we had little warning, the hotel staff gathered everyone on the ground floor into the centre of the lobby away from windows."

I take a breath before continuing. "Ever since that day I have been terrified of thunderstorms. As soon as I hear thunder, I seek shelter under a bed or in a closet, afraid of what would happen if the storm produced a tornado. I don't want to go through that experience again."

Blake stares at me, processing my words. "Wow." He looks away from me for a second before turning back to me. "Listen, I'm sorry for yelling at you earlier. I didn't mean to. If I had known about your phobia, I wouldn't have given you a hard time."

I turn to him, giving him a half smile to show I had forgiven him.

"Are you sure it's just astraphobia you have? Do you have lilasophobia as well?"

I stare at him with a puzzle look. It was a fear I haven't heard of before. "Lilasophobia?"

"It's a fear of tornadoes or hurricanes. I'm not saying you have it, but I'm just curious if you do have it. It's the most severe type of astraphobia. From the way you acted out there today, I would say lilasophobia."

I shrug. "Maybe. I'm not sure. The doctor only diagnosed me with astraphobia."

Blake nods. "Okay. Well, I guess that makes sense since like you said, tornadoes aren't something that happens a lot in Australia."

"Have you been in a tornado besides the ones you chase?"

He nods. "For a while I grew up in Missouri. I have been in a few tornadoes there. In high school my dad got a job in Colorado. Occasionally there are tornadoes there, but not many. Tommy happens to be my neighbour. Your Mom lives near the border of Colorado and Kansas."

"Don't you get scared chasing them?"

"Scared? Yeah, all the time. Tornadoes are so unpredictable that you never know what's going to happen. From the distance they are an amazing piece of nature. Up close they are deadly."

"Do you know if we are storm chasing tomorrow?"

Before Blake could answer my question, the door opens and Tommy walks out of mine and Mum's room.

"Hey, what are you two up to?" he asks.

"Just talking," Blake answers.

He smiles at us. "Okay, well don't stay up too late. We have a big day tomorrow. We're hitting the road early."

My stomach twists into knots, making me feel nausea at the thought of storm chasing tomorrow. Why didn't anyone understand how I felt, especially Mum? This is not how I planned my vacation with her. How am I supposed to catch up the last three years of our lives with her?

I get up so Tommy could enter his room. I said good night to both of the guys, and enter my own. As I enter, I couldn't make any eye contact with my mother. Looking at her would make me want to yell at her for breaking her promise. It wasn't the right place to argue, especially when people in other rooms will hear.

I say goodnight to her, crawling into bed while she stayed on her laptop. I lay there, listening to Mum tap on the keyboard or the click of the mouse. Eventually she crawls into the bed beside me half an hour later.

Chapter 6

I lie there in the darkness, listening to Mum's soft snoring. I'm unable to get any sleep as my mind constantly replays today's events, and what could happen tomorrow.

I don't remember drifting off to sleep. When Mum shakes me gently in the morning, I regretted not getting enough sleep, no matter how much my mind kept me awake. Groaning, I get up to see the sun rising as the light sneaks its way through the closed curtain. It was five thirty in the morning. Mum said that Tommy wanted to make sure everything is pack in the SUV, and then we were going to go out for breakfast before heading on the road again. I have no idea where we are going today, but I really wish we could do something other than storm chase.

Mum disappears to the bathroom to change. Rather than getting change myself, I grab Mum's laptop from the table near the television. I sit down with it, opening up to see what the weather forecast would be for today. It was sunny in the area we were, but I still had no idea which way we would be travelling to. According to the radar there were a couple of storm cells to the northeast of Oklahoma, crossing the borders of Kansas, Missouri and Arkansas. A tornado watch was also issue for the thunderstorms, and I pray silently to myself that no tornadoes form from any of them.

I spend a bit of time glancing at the screen, studying the radar, when Mum walks out. I close the screen, thinking she would tell me off for using her computer without her consent. But she doesn't yell. Instead she smiles, and walks over to me.

"You aren't dress yet, Charli," she tells me.

"Yeah, sorry." I put the laptop down on the bed and stood up. "I was just checking the weather. I often do that every morning before I get dress or leave the house."

"It's okay." She sits down on the bed, pulling the laptop into her lap. "It's just that Tommy will be coming in soon so we can discuss our plans for today. I will warn you now, he isn't a morning person."

I nod, and grab some clean clothes out of my bag.

"How is the weather forecast for the day?" she asks, opening up the laptop.

"Are you storm chasing again?"

Mum looks up from the screen, her blue-green eyes meeting mine. Guilt appears in them, but doesn't seem to really care how I feel. "Yes, we are going storm chasing today. I know I'd promised I wouldn't, but I need to work, Charli. The season is almost over, and then we can spend time together."

I bite my lip as I shake my head. "No. You won't have time for me until I decide to leave."

"Charli, I know you're angry, but I really need to work. This is my job."

I head towards the bathroom to change. Before I enter, I turn to Mum. "Even if it is your job, I'm sure you could take a couple of days off. You don't have to chase every storm cell that shows up on the radar."

"I know, but it's an agreement Tommy and I made at the start of the season to catch as many tornadoes as we can. The season is almost over and there is still a lot of data we need to collect. Even if I take a break from chasing, I won't be satisfied with my work until I have got what I need."

I shake my head, frowning. "It's nice to know you're so committed to your own work than your own daughter."

I see the hurt in my mother's eyes, but I have no sympathy for her if I say any harsh words. She knows whatever I'm saying is true.

"Charli, please don't act like this."

I ignore her and enter the bathroom. I lock the door. Mum knocks, asking me to open it, but I don't. I rest my back against the door for a second, listening to Mum as she continues on.

"Charli, I need you to understand why I'm doing all of this. I want you to know how much I love you. Don't think you are not wanted here, because you are. I'm glad you're here."

Bull crap, I want to say.

Instead of saying it, I move away from the door, staying silent so I don't have to argue with her. I undressed as she continues to beg me to open up so we can talk, but I don't. Her voice goes silent, and for a moment I thought maybe she had finally gotten the message that I didn't want to speak to her. But then I hear her talking to someone in our room. I frown when I hear Tommy's voice who had come in to discuss which storm they will be chasing today.

I finish getting ready before joining the others, who were sitting on the bed with the laptop sitting in front of them. Tommy and

Mum discuss what their plans were for today. Blake is behind them, peeking over their shoulders, sitting on his knees.

I stand nearby, listening to them as I pack away my things into my suitcase. They talk using weather terms I couldn't understand. They discuss that the supercell forming over where the borders of the states Oklahoma, Kansas, and Missouri come together has a higher chance of dropping a funnel than the supercell forming over Arkansas. I hope no funnel will be drop, and all it will be is a thunderstorm. I don't want a repeat of what happened yesterday.

"Right, let's get going," Tommy announces, getting off the bed. "We will stop to get breakfast, and then we will start heading northeast of here."

Blake and Tommy leave the room to fletch their belongings. There wasn't much to pack up, only a few of Mum's clothes that still needed to be packed away. I had everything I needed, so I picked up my luggage to meet everyone out in the car park.

Mum calls me just as I reach the door. Rolling my eyes, I turn to face her.

"Charli, before the rest of this vacation continues, and before we set out on the road, we need to talk."

I shake my head. "No. What's the point? You won't hear what I have to say. All I wanted was to catch up, but instead you choose to work. Ever since you began studying meteorology, that's all you really care about."

"Charli –"

I hold my hand up to signal her to stop. "Just drop it, Mum."

I walk out of the room before Mum could say anything. I stroll across the car park, and lean my back up against the SUV's boot. Since it was so early in the morning, the motel felt lifeless with no movement at all. Everyone is probably still fast asleep as its six o'clock, and here we are about to start the day driving across the states to chase storms. I much rather choose the sleeping option. In the distance I can hear the faint sound of the early morning traffic on a highway that's near the motel.

"You look tired," Blake's voice interrupts my thoughts. "Didn't you get any sleep?"

I look over in his direction as he approaches me with two duffel bags, one over his shoulder and holds the other, and his camera bag in his other hand. I see Tommy in the distance, standing outside our rooms, discussing something with Mum. From the look on her face, she looks as if she had told him about me.

"Yeah, I had trouble sleeping," I answer Blake.

He puts the bags beside our feet. "Well, it's a long road trip so you will be able to catch up on some sleep along the way." He pulls out a set of keys from his pocket and unlocks the back boot with the key remote.

"How long will it take to get where we need to go?"

He opens up the boot. "From here to where the borders of Oklahoma, Kansas, and Missouri meet, it will take us six hours."

"*Six hours?!*" Was he joking? How could Mum and Tommy travel that distance for a tornado, even if it was a part of their job? I couldn't imagine travelling so many miles each day for a storm.

Blake reaches for my bag and places it in the back. "Yeah, some days are long from all of the driving."

"I don't know how you guys can travel so much. Don't you get any free time to yourselves?"

"Of course we do. Some days there are no chasing at all."

"I hope today is the last. I seriously don't want to do anymore chasing."

Blake stares at me, chewing the inside of his mouth. He then glances over where Tommy was walking towards reception to check us out, and Mum walks towards us. He turns back to me. "Listen, Charli. I know you don't like doing this storm chasing stuff, how you really want to catch up with your Mom, and how you are terrified of storms. Even if this vacation is not what you expect, it could help your relationship with her."

I stare at him, puzzle. "How will it help with our relationship?"

"Well, for instant you could discover something about her that you never really knew before. All she really wants is for you to take an interest in something she does. And even if you're terrified of storms, doing these chases is a good way to get over your fear by putting yourself out there."

Mum walks over to us, smiling, like nothing happened between us this morning. She places her luggage into the boot, along with Tommy's things and then closes it. She turns to us. "Ready?"

"All set, April." Blake smiles brightly.

"Great, well Tommy should be out in a sec and then we can get something to eat."

She turns away, climbing into the front passenger seat. Tommy walks out of reception, heading towards us.

"Please don't freak out with the next storm," Blake tells me. "Just give this storm chasing a chance. And as much as you're angry with your mother, give her a chance to make up for lost time. Not every day you get to have this opportunity to chase after tornadoes." He smiles at me and then gets into the car.

I take in the things he said, wondering if he was right. Even if he was, I couldn't understand how the chase was going to help with my fear or my relationship with my mother. We don't seem to understand each other. Mum didn't want to listen to half of the things I wanted. It was like she didn't care anymore. She acts like I'm not even her daughter sometimes.

Before Tommy has a chance to tell me to get into the car as he gets closer, I hop into the vehicle, dreading another day of storm chasing.

Chapter 7

A news broadcast was playing when we entered a diner, showing a twister ripping through a small town in Nebraska around four thirty this morning. It was hard to spot it the dark, but power flashes showed the outline of the EF2 tornado on camera. Mum, Tommy and Blake were focus on the news broadcast while I read the menu, not wanting to watch the television.

A waitress stands beside our table, greeting us in a thick southern accent. She takes down our order on a small notepad. As soon as she walks away with our order, Mum and Tommy discuss the Nebraska tornado between themselves, as well as the storm we will chase today. Blake and I sit there in silence across from each other. He watches me, glancing over at Tommy and Mum every few seconds.

Our breakfast is soon served and we eat quickly before setting out onto the road again. I listen to music on my phone as I gaze out of the window as we pass through small towns, cities and farms until we reach the highway to take us towards the northeast of the state of Oklahoma that borders Kansas and Missouri. The music helps me to keep my mind off everything.

I dose off to sleep without even realising I had until Blake wakes me when Tommy pulls over at a rest stop. We stay there for ten minutes to stretch our legs and have a toilet break before hitting the road again.

When we were near the Missouri-Oklahoma border, Tommy pulls over on the side of the road so he and Mum could observe the clouds that were turning a dark blue. I stay in the car as the others get out. Blake takes his camera and films the lightning strikes. Inside the car I could hear the faint sounds of thunder rumbling in the distance. The road was wet so it had been raining here earlier. I could see the grey lines from the rain falling from the clouds in the distance.

Through the window, I watch Mum and Tommy discuss which direction was best to travel in. Tommy points out to a tint of green clouds to the northeast and decided to head in the direction. The three of them hop back into the car. Tommy pulls back onto the highway, continuing to head east. Mum turns on the radio to listen for any updates on the weather.

The radio issues a tornado warning for our area.

My stomach turns into knots. "So there is definitely going to be a tornado?" I ask.

Mum turns in her seat to look back at me, surprise I have spoken at all through the trip. I was surprise myself I had spoken, but I was curious about the clouds Tommy had mentioned being green. From what I knew about clouds being green is that it often means severe weather, usually hail, but sometimes it didn't mean anything at all.

"We don't know yet. There is nothing on the radar yet to indicate if there is going to be a tornado or not. A tornado warning has been issue so most likely there will be one." She turns to look at her computer. "I don't see any hook echoes just yet."

We continue driving along, passing the city of Joplin until we came to an exit on the interstate for a road that travels to the northeast. We watch the clouds as we drive, looking for anything to indicate that a tornado was going to form soon. I stare out the window myself, but not watching for tornadoes. I watch the clouds, wondering what they will do. Tears fill my eyes and I hid my face from the others so they couldn't see.

As we reach the town of Hoxton, the rain pattered down heavily. Thankfully with the car in motion, I couldn't hear the thunder. I had to turn away from the window so I wouldn't panic. If I was with Dad, I would be in the backseat my now, sobbing until the storm is over. Here I couldn't do it. Not when Mum, Tommy and Blake doesn't understand my phobia the way Dad does. I stare down at my lap, biting down on my lip, as the others got excited about lightning strikes ripping through the sky.

"Hey, there's a funnel to the southeast," Blake says suddenly.

I don't look, but I know the others are. Tommy pulls to the side of the road, and the three of them get out of the car to observe the funnel cloud Blake had spotted. I unbuckle my seat belt and then move to the front seat where I could get a glance at the radar on my mother's laptop. I see a lot of red in our area, as well as a few purple spots within the red. I knew the red meant heavy rain, but I wasn't sure what purple meant, but I knew it was something that probably wouldn't be good.

I began feeling nausea when I spot a hook echo on the radar. I look up and glance out of the window, looking in the direction of the funnel cloud Blake spotted. The clouds were no longer a dark blue like it was from the distance. They were a dark grey colour now that we were directly underneath the storm. I see the funnel cloud in a field hiding behind a row of trees. I wonder if that's the funnel the radar has detected.

And then I hear it. The siren warning a tornado is either still developing or is on the ground. I place my hands over my ears and squeeze my eyes shut tightly.

"Please stop, please stop," I mumble to myself like the siren could hear me.

It doesn't stop. Even with my ears covered, I could still hear it ringing in my ears. Tears manage to escape my eyes, and before I know it, I'm sobbing uncontrollably that my body shakes. I promise myself I wouldn't do this. Not while I'm here with the others, but that promise went out the door as soon I heard the siren. All I wanted was for it to stop.

"Do you know if it has touch ground yet?" I hear Mum yell over the siren.

"I can't tell through the trees," Tommy yells back. "We need to travel further up the road, find a clear opening to get a better look."

I hear them hurrying along the grass to get back in the SUV.

"Charli?" Mum asks with concern.

I feel a pair of hands resting on my waist. I know they aren't Mum's. They're too big to be hers. I hear Blake's voice telling Tommy to go, and then telling Mum that he has me, asking her to film footage for him. He pulls me towards him, sitting me on his lap. I bury my face into his chest, wetting his shirt as he rubs a hand over my back, telling me it's okay.

Something hits the roof hard. Tommy curses as something smashes the windscreen. I place a hand on Blake's chest, clenching his shirt tightly in my hand.

"Damn, look at the size of the hail," Blake says. "April, are you getting this on camera?"

"I'm getting it, Blake. Tommy, turn right up ahead," Mum says.

The hail continues to belt down heavily on top of us until Tommy gets a couple of metres down the road when it stops.

"No, no, no!" Mum cries. "Damn it. It disappeared."

The car slows to a halt.

"What does the radar say?" Tommy asks.

"A hook echo is visible, and it says it's forming right where we are. Do you see anything, Tommy? Is there any visibility on a wall cloud or anything rotating? What about you, Blake? What do you see?"

"I don't see anything on my side," Tommy answers.

"Neither can I," Blake replies.

A door opens and someone gets out, follow by a second person. I hear Mum and Tommy discussing which way the wind is blowing. Tommy suggests maybe heading north, but Mum disagrees.

"Charli, hey look at me," Blake tells me.

I shake my head. "No, I can't. If I look up, I will glance outside and I really don't want to do that. I will panic."

He places his hands on either side of my face and gently lifts my head up towards him. He brushes his thumbs over my cheeks, wiping away the tears. As I stare at him, I notice he has specks of green amongst his brown eyes, full of concern.

"Hey, you don't have to look outside," he tells me. "Just keep your eyes focus on me, okay? Forget what's going on outside."

As he says that, thunder claps loudly, making me jump. Blake grabs my hands, squeezing them.

"What do you normally do when there's a storm?" he continues.

"I hide until it's over."

Mum and Tommy mumble something about not being able to see a wall cloud. Blake looks outside for a brief second before turning back to me.

"Come step outside for a second," he suggests.

I shake my head. "No. I can't."

"It's okay, Charli. I know you're scared, but the weather is something you have to face every day. I will be right with you when we step out."

"The storm isn't over."

"I know, and it might be a while before it is over. Listen, you're safe from the storm, okay? Nothing is going to happen to you. I promise. Think of something that makes you happy to keep your mind off the storm. What makes you happy, Charli?"

I remember the programs I had to attend to help with my phobia. One of the ideal activities to help me keep calm in the storm was to think of something to make me feel happy; forget that the storm was outside. It never helped me much. None of the activities suggested helped me with my fear.

I shake my head. "Please don't try that on me. I have been to classes to help with my fear, and it never helped."

He nods slowly. "Okay, well I'm going to get you to step outside. It's raining, and there is some lightning around also, but I promise that the storm will not do any harm to you."

I nod, but I wasn't fully convinced with his plan. He reaches for the door handle and opens the door. I force myself to look outside, seeing the grass covered in white hail stones the size of baseballs, making it look like it had snowed.

I take in a deep breath, doing some breathing exercises to help me stay calm. The rain is still pouring down, drenching me instantly, and I couldn't understand how Tommy and Mum could stand out here, willing to get soak as they observe the clouds. The wind starts to pick up. My stomach starts to twist and turn, knowing something will happen soon. A flash of lightning rips through the sky. I was about to take shelter inside the SUV to escape the thunder, but Blake takes my hand, squeezing it tightly as the thunder claps loudly.

He whispers in my ear, his breath tickling my ear. "Remember, I'm here, okay? The storm is harmful. You're safe."

I repeat his words softly to myself, taking deep breaths as I do so, trying to forget that the storm is around me.

"Right, we need to head north," Tommy says.

"Are you sure?" Blake asks. "I though April said the hook echo was forming here."

"I thought so too," Mum replies. "But it doesn't seem like there will be one. There is no wall cloud. The other funnel that had formed wasn't a tornado at all."

I look up at the sky, scanning the clouds, unsure what I was looking for. I watch the clouds as they move fast. I then notice some rotation across the road from us. I squeeze Blake's hand.

"I think we are underneath the wall cloud," I say.

Chapter 8

Mum follows my gaze to where I have spotted the rotating clouds above us. She smiles at me. "Good work, Charli." She turns to the guys. "Let's get back into the SUV before this storm does produce a funnel and drops right on us."

We scramble into the vehicle. I was the first to climb in, curling up in the backseat as the others follow. The nausea feeling in my stomach worsens, but now was not the time to be sick.

"Which way do you want to head to?" Tommy asks. "North or south?"

"South," Mum answers. "Let's go further down this road and pull over so we're able to observe the funnel and figure out which direction it's going to head."

Tommy starts the car and travels further down the road, speeding. Half a mile down he does a U-turn where we are now facing a visible funnel cloud forming right where we were before. Both Mum and Tommy jump out to observe the funnel. Mum films it with Blake's camera as he tries to get me out of the car once more.

It takes him about five minutes to convince me it's safe to step out of the vehicle. When I do step out it's not because he convinced me it was safe, but because I couldn't hold onto the sickening feeling inside my stomach any longer. I push him out of my way and run over to the wire fence beside the road, vomiting onto the grass.

"Are you alright, Charli?" Mum asks as she walks over to me.

I wipe my mouth with the back of my hand. "I'm fine, Mum."

She gives me a half smile and then turns her attention back to the funnel cloud, which is almost on the ground. Blake grabs his camera from Mum and keeps it focus on the funnel. When no one is looking, I hop back into the SUV to get out of the cold rain. I buckle my seat belt knowing that very soon we will be moving again.

I glance through the window to see that the funnel was inches to the ground. Mum is on the phone, reporting the tornado to the National Weather Service. Within minutes of getting off the phone, Mum's laptop has a tornado warning alert.

The others continue to observe the tornado, warning any passing motorists as they ignore the developing tornado. Some speed down the road to get by before it does touch ground, while others parked on the side of the road behind us, waiting for any instructions we give them so they are safe. Tommy didn't like it much that they were parking behind us, especially when he and Mum were unsure which way the tornado will travel and we may have to move in a hurry if it does head in our direction.

As soon as it touches ground, Mum, Tommy and Blake swiftly gets into the SUV before the winds pick up the debris of dust and grass in the field. The wire fence wobbles side to side until it's blown completely to the side. Up ahead I see the fence snap, getting thrown in the air by the winds. The twister then moves across the field, heading northwest.

Tommy turns onto the road, speeding to keep up with the tornado.

I turn to look in the opposite direction so I couldn't watch the vortex move across the field, heading towards properties. Watching it would only bring back terrifying memories that I no longer wanted to remember. The constant excitement I could hear in the others' voices made me feel sick. How could they be excited over this?

"Are you able to get ahead of it, Tommy?" Mum asks.

"I can try," he answers. "It's not going to be easy with traffic." He overtakes two cars ahead of us and quickly moves into the right lane before he had a head on collision as a pickup truck comes towards us.

"It looks like it's going to cross the road up ahead, maybe even cross the freeway that's just north northwest of here."

"Oh crap. Hopefully the freeway is not too busy today."

Tommy speeds to keep up with the tornado, dodging other motorist in the safest way possible. Mum tells him to get off this road and to turn left onto a road that was going to intercept the tornado's path.

I grab hold of the door handle, hanging on so tightly that my knuckles turn white. I close my eyes, silently praying to myself for all of this to be over in a jiffy. Maybe the tornado won't be on the ground for too long.

The windows of Mum's and Blake's were wind down for a brief moment. The whistling and howling winds blow through, sending debris and rain our way. Unable to keep the windows down any longer, they wind it up as the rain became heavy, so heavy that Tommy could no longer see the road. Blake and Mum no longer had visual on the tornado as it became rain wrapped.

Tommy turns onto a road, hoping to get in front of the twister where they could place the probe in the path before it crosses the freeway. Mum hoped once Tommy turned onto the new road that she could get a clear visual on the vortex, but it was still completely rain wrapped. We couldn't even see any debris. We drive pass a row of trees on the side of the road, completely blocking our view of the tornado.

"April, we need to turn around," Tommy says. "With the tornado being rain wrapped, it's going to be too dangerous for us to try and intercept."

"We could still do it, Tommy," Mum says.

Tommy shakes his head. "No. I'm not putting any of us in danger."

Knowing I wasn't supposed to unbuckle my seat belt, I did anyway, scooting over to Blake. He glances at me as I sat closer to him, feeling a sudden need of security as I hold onto his arm and rest my head on his shoulder. The trees were swaying violently in the wind, and looks as it might snap in half or be pulled out of the ground with its roots still intact.

"I'm pulling over, April," Tommy says. "I can no longer see the road through this rain."

Just as he pulls the vehicle to the side of the road, two trees were pulled out of the ground with the roots still intact were thrown, blocking the road in front of us. I hold onto Blake's arm tightly. He lets out a soft groan as my finger nails dig into his arm, but he doesn't say anything about me letting go.

The car shakes, hearing the roaring winds right in front of us. Tree branches and other debris hit us as the tornado strikes a property that's surrounded by trees. We weren't sure how close the tornado was, only that it was right in front of us, about to cross the road. Not taking any risk of staying too close to the rain wrapped funnel, Tommy shifts the gear into reverse.

He puts his foot down to move backwards just as an unknown object hits the windscreen, shattering it to pieces. Quickly, we shield our faces from the glass. While everyone stays calm, I scream as the wind whistles through the open window, glass, leaves and small pieces of debris flies our way. Blake pushes me down on the backseat, leaning his body over me to shield me from the debris. Mum and Tommy leans forward in their seats, covering their heads.

I squeeze my eyes shut as Blake whispers in my ear that everything was going to be alright, but that's not what my mind was telling me. Within seconds the wind subsides as the tornado passes us.

"Is everyone alright?" Tommy asks.

Mum answers yes. Blake looks down at me and answers yes. He continues to stare at me, not making an effort to push me away as I continued to cling on him for security even though the tornado had passed us.

"Charli, are you alright?" Mum asks me.

Turning my eyes away from Blake, I look over at Mum. She had a cut above her left eyebrow, blood gushing down. I push Blake off me and sit up in a hurry. "Mum, you're bleeding!"

Mum gives me a small smile. "I know, sweetie. I'm fine."

I shake my head, leaning forward in my seat. "No, Mum. You're not fine."

"April, check the glove compartment," Tommy says, who has a cut on his right cheek. "There should be some napkins in there." He turns to look at Blake and I. "Are you both sure you're okay?"

Blake answers yes, while I nod slowly, watching Mum as she opens the glove compartment, grabbing some napkins. She hands some to Tommy to press against his cheek, and she presses some against her eyebrow, blood immediately turning the white napkins crimson.

Chapter 9

The emergency services soon arrive shortly after the tornado had struck. It had stopped raining, and we had a better view of the destruction the tornado had left behind. Everywhere I look amongst the scatter debris I could hear sirens in the distance, or someone needing assistant. Staring at the aftermath I wondered to myself where do the residents pick up their lives where they last left them?

I should walk around and help the others to look for anyone who could be trapped beneath the rubble. Instead, I sit at the back of an ambulance, watching Tommy search the rubble while Mum talk to an old lady who was holding onto her Jack Russell. Only two properties on the street we were on was destroyed, while other properties had mild or no damage at all. A paramedic had wrapped a blanket around me to keep warm after being soaked from the rain. He kept asking me if I had any injuries, but I blank out from his words. All I could think about is our near-death experience. It brought back the memories of when my parents and I were in the hotel and a tornado had struck it. I really don't want to ever go through another experience like that again.

"Hey, how are you doing?" Blake walks over to me. I was watching him earlier filming the devastation with his camera.

I give him a half smile, but don't say anything.

He sits down beside me, resting his camera in his lap. "Your mom said we will be leaving soon."

I nod slowly.

We sit there in silence, staring at the rubble.

"How do these people know where to pick up their lives where they last left it, starting over after losing everything?" I ask.

Blake shrugs, shaking his head. "I don't know. I have gone through this a couple of times myself. As soon as you know that your family and friends are alright, you start to clean what you can. Sometimes it's pure luck when some of your prize possessions aren't damage. Starting over is the hardest thing ever, but the most important thing is you're alive and so is the others around you."

"Please tell me we aren't chasing anymore tornadoes. I can't bear to be caught in another one."

Blake scratches his head. "Well, I don't know what tomorrow will bring, but I know we won't be doing any more chasing today. Tommy has to find a place to get the windshield fix."

"I just want it to end."

Blake reaches over and takes my hand, squeezing it. I glance down at it before glancing up at him.

"Listen, I know you're terrified of storms," he says. "And I know I told you earlier before we went on this chase how important it is to expose yourself to these storms. I know how terrifying it must feel and how difficult it is to face your fear. The weather is part of our everyday life whether you like it or not. I would say you have nothing to worry about. Not every supercell produces a tornado."

I nod. "I know. I'm just scared of what happened, and I don't want to go through it again."

"You live in Australia, right? How many tornadoes do they normally have in a year?"

I shrug. "I don't know. I know there has been a few, but they don't really get reported as big headlines, unless it was something really major."

"Exactly. Some tornadoes don't get reported. Australia has an average of sixteen tornadoes a year, maybe more that storm chasers don't know about or haven't been reported. Here in the United States, there's an average of over a thousand and two hundred tornadoes, maybe more. About an average of a hundred and twenty-five strikes Texas while an average of fifty-eight strikes Oklahoma. So if you look at the average of what the United States gets, you're pretty lucky to be living in Australia."

"What's the average of the other states?"

Blake shrugs. "I'm not sure. That's just some facts I found once when Tommy wanted me to research tornadoes before I started the internship, that way I had a better understanding about them. Maybe researching tornadoes or about other storms will give you a better understanding, and help with your fear. Being here on the chase may help to conquer your fear."

I think about the last thing he had said. I wasn't even sure to believe him. How could being out on the chase help conquer my fear of storms? Wouldn't it worsen? Since being on the chase, I have been in two near death situations and that has not helped my phobia. I know there are so many different treatments to help face your phobias and then eventually get over them. For me I found none of them had worked. Maybe the treatments work for some people, but none of the support groups I have been to has helped to recover from my fear. And even if Blake thinks exposing myself to storms or joining the chase would help with my fear, I doubt it will.

I was just about to ask him how it would benefit me, when Mum calls us over, telling us it was time to hit the road again.

Blake stands up and looks down at me. "Has your mother ever told you the reason why she took up storm chasing or why she studied meteorology?"

I nod, standing up and removing the blanket from around me, folding it up neatly. "Yeah, Mum has always been passionate about storms. When I was younger, she used to sit outside and watch a storm develop. She wanted me to take an interest in meteorology too, but I never did."

Blake shakes his head. "No. That's not the real reason why she did it."

I stare at him, confused. How would he know the real reason why, and not Dad or me? I'm her daughter, not some stranger. Shouldn't Dad and I have the right to know the truth?

"What is the reason?" I ask, placing the blanket on the floor of the ambulance.

"Blake, Charli, come on," Mum calls us. "Let's get going."

"Just a minute!" Blake calls back. He turns to me. "The real reason she took on this job was because she was terrified of losing you and your dad. She realised how deadly tornadoes were. Since the incident that almost claimed your life, she has become so fascinated by tornadoes, wanting to know everything about them. Like other meteorologist, she wanted to know how the inside of a tornado works. We pretty much know how it works with all of the data we have collected over the years, but still there's a lot of things we may not know about them. April wanted to be a part of helping better warning systems so people are able to get to safety quicker, which has improved because of social media. Maybe even invent something that could detect a tornado earlier before it touches on the ground."

I stare at him, unsure whether or not if I should be proud of my mother or if I should be angry. I look over at her where she and Tommy were speaking to the old lady with her dog. The moment my eyes land on her, the anger I felt for the last four years after she left me and Dad kicks in. My head felt like it was going to explode at any second, wanting to scream. Mum lied. She lied to both dad and me about the reasons why she wanted to study meteorology, for the reasons why she wanted to come to the States and study tornadoes. She never mentioned any of this to us.

Blake turns to head over to Mum and Tommy.

I clench my fist together as I follow him, hesitating whether if I should say something; ask him more questions about what he knew about my mother that I didn't already know. Why did she lie? Was storm chasing really her lifelong dream? Why would she tell a stranger, who she had only known for a short time, about the real reason why she ditched her life as a nurse to become a meteorologist, but couldn't tell her husband of eighteen years or only child about why she had made this decision?

And if she had been terrified of losing us in the tornado that almost took our lives, did she realise she had already lost Dad and me since she began studying meteorology?

"Where are we heading to?" Blake asks as we join Tommy and Mum.

As soon as we join them, I make eye contact with the ground so I couldn't look at my mother. She will see the anger in my eyes and right now wasn't the place for us to argue about the past.

"We are heading to Wiley just outside of Joplin," Tommy answers. "There's a windshield repair place there. We will also spend the night in the town."

"Are we chasing more tornadoes?" I couldn't help asking.

"We will see how the weather is tomorrow. For now, we will rest up for tonight."

***

Mum and Tommy left as soon as they book a room at the motel, heading to a repair place for the windscreen. Blake disappears to the room he is sharing with Tommy on the bottom floor while I stay in the one I'm sharing with Mum on the second floor. I take a shower to wash off the dirt on my skin.

A knock comes from the door as soon as I step out of the shower. I yell out that I would be in a second, knowing it was most likely Blake, quickly changing into fresh clothes. Once changed, I answer the door to find Blake standing there.

"Hey, are you doing anything?" he asks.

I shake my head. "Not at the moment. Why?"

"Well, I figure since April and Tommy is getting the car fix, maybe we could hang out."

I smile, liking the idea. It was better than being stuck in this motel room alone. I wasn't even sure what to do while I wait for Mum to return. "What do you have in mind?"

"I'm thinking of visiting the library. There is one not far from here. Would you like to come?"

I answer yes.

We catch the bus that would take us to the public library, which was fifteen minutes away from the motel.

When we arrive, Blake kindly asks the librarian where the books on meteorology are, and she directs him where to go. He takes my hand and then leads me in the direction the librarian had directed us to. I don't ask him about the reason why he is leading me to the meteorology section. Straight away I know he is probably going to find something that would help me with my fear. The thought of it made me feel sick in the stomach.

He finds the section and then scans the shelf for the book he was looking for. He pulls out a thin book off the shelf on tornadoes, opening it and flips through it. He turns to me.

"Here," he says. "You should read through this. It's a short book with a lot of pictures and a few sentences so you don't have to worry about reading too much. It basically gives you all of the basic facts you need to know on tornadoes."

I stare at the book in my hands with a picture of a tornado destroying a building on the cover. I look up at Blake. How can he expect me to read this or even think it would help with my fear? I can't even watch a news broadcast when they report on tornadoes.

"Why do you want me to read through this?" I knew the answer since he had told me earlier about researching storms to understand them more and help with my phobia. It was nice to know he wanted to help, but I seriously doubt his idea would ever help me.

It was like he knew what I was thinking. "You know very well why I want you to read it. I can't guarantee this will help you with your fear, but maybe learning the facts could help you to understand these storms more when we are on a chase."

I look down at the cover, my stomach twisting at the sight of the picture. I shake my head. "No, I can't read this, Blake." I look at him so we are now making eye contact. "Look, it's nice to know that you would really like to help me with my phobia, but I don't think this is really going to help me at all."

I hand the book back to him, and he takes it. As I turn away, he grabs my arm.

"Wait. Don't go just yet," he tells me. "Please give this a chance. Try and see if reading through this will help you. If not, then I promise you I won't force you with anything that will help you recover from your fear."

I think for a second and then nod. "Okay."

Blake gives me a smile, takes my hand and leads me to a corner in the back beside the shelves where there were some black bean bags. I wasn't sure if the bean bags were a comfortable place to read, but at least we were alone, away from the other people in the library.

We sit down closely together. Blake opens the book, going through it as he explains the facts to me. I stare at the pictures, as well as the words, reading the information for myself. Occasionally I look up at Blake as he speaks, which makes my heart flutter in my chest.

When we get to the end of the book, he closes it, staring at me. "So? What do you think?"

I shrug. "I don't know."

"Just tell me the information was useful to you."

"They were interesting and you explained it really well. Thanks, Blake." I give him a warm smile to show my appreciation.

He returns it. "Promise me when we go on another chase once the car is fixed, that you will make an effort not to be scared. I want you to be able to see the beauty of the storm besides the disaster side of it."

"I'm pretty sure you made me promise that, and I broke it."

"Yeah, I may have mentioned it, but it doesn't matter. Even if you did break it, you can start over again. I completely understand if this phobia is something you can't get over so easily. I'm terrified of heights and I have never been able to get over it. Look, tornado season is almost over. Tommy and April are going to be on the road for maybe a couple of more weeks. How long are you visiting your mom for?"

"I'm here for two weeks."

"Do you think you're able to handle the next two weeks of storm chasing?"

He is kidding, right? Hasn't he seen how I have acted for the two days? There is no way I can handle another two weeks of storm chasing.

"Blake, I already cannot handle it."

Blake stares at me, and then down at the book. He stares at it before turning back to me, reaching out for my hand and squeezes it. "I will help you get over this phobia of yours. It's okay to be scared when you're chasing tornadoes. I get scared all the time. They're unpredictable, but at the same time you can't let your phobia get the best of you. If you do, you could put yourself and the rest of the team in danger like you did yesterday when you panicked, running into the path of an oncoming tornado. We would have been able to get out of the way of it if you didn't pulled that stunt. A tornado cannot do any harm if you just stay out of its way. And if you do end up being in the middle of one, as long as you get yourself to safety in time, you will be fine. Other storms cannot harm you unless you put yourself in danger, like stand out in the open near something that will attract lightning."

I knew Blake was right, but convincing myself was another thing. Each time I have been to therapy to help me to recover from the phobia, I only had to remember a flashback of that day on our vacation to make me realise why I hated storms.

I guess I could give storm chasing a go. There is no harm is finding another way of helping with my fear. There was no use saying it won't help if I don't try.

"Okay, I will see how I go with facing my fear," I say.

He smiles. "That's great. I will be with you at all times, unless I run off to film footage. But I will be there. Just take deep breaths and everything will be fine."

I thank him one last time before we leave the library, heading to a nearby café to eat something for lunch.

Chapter 10

Mum was sitting on the bed with her laptop when Blake and I walk into the room. She looks up from the papers she had in her hands. She smiles at both Blake and me, greeting us. Blake returns the greeting before leaving us to disappear to his room.

"What did you and Blake get up to while Tommy and I fixed the SUV?" Mum asks me as I close the door.

I walk over to join her on the double Queen size bed. "We went to the library before getting something to eat."

She sets the papers down on the sheets beside her laptop, which she closes so I don't see the radar on the screen. My stomach twists into knots, wondering what the weather will be the next day and if we are going on any chases. Mum turns to me, continuing to smile. "You and Blake are getting along well."

"He has been really nice to me and trying to help me get over my fear."

"That's good to hear. Look, I know I'm dragging you along with these chases when I know how much you dislike storms, but I need to collect more data. The season is almost over, and we haven't been able to be successful with what we want. We are trying to find the perfect way to intercept the tornado. Once we finish with this season, Tommy and I will be working and planning what we will be doing for next year. Have I told you about what Tommy and I planning to do next season?"

I nod. "Yeah, you said something about getting closer to it so the winds won't be able to pick you up."

Mum smiles. "You should come visit and join us for the next season. I'm not sure yet if Blake will be joining us, but you're more than welcome to. Our next vehicle will hopefully be safer next year. Some storm chasing teams have already invested in making their vehicle safe enough to intercept a tornado. The vehicle will have bulletproof windows, steel armoured and grappling claws to anchor us to the ground, which will be able to stabilise us up to 165 miles per hour winds. We will mostly be able to intercept EF0 to EF3. EF4 and EF5 are too strong for us to intercept."

I pretend to listen when really I couldn't care less. Even if she did want me to join her chases next year, or if Blake does successfully help me get over my fear of storms, I still wanted no part of my mother's career.

I don't give her a yes or no answer if I would definitely come visit her again. Instead I ask her how the wound above her forehead is. The good thing was it wasn't a deep cut so it didn't need stitches. It was just above her left eyebrow, red around the cut that will probably heal in a few weeks.

"It's fine," she replies. "It hurts a little, but it's all good." She gives me a small smile.

We sit there in silence. I have been out of touch with my mother for so long, I had no idea what to speak to her about. And even if I did have something to say, would Mum want to listen without using some excuse to say she had to work?

Mum stands up, grabbing her laptop and the papers.

"What are those papers for?" I ask.

Mum puts the laptop down on the cupboard beside the TV. "Oh, it's just some stuff for work." She turns to me, tucking a strand of her hair behind her ear. "Would you like to go out for dinner tonight? It will just be you and me."

I smile, agreeing to do so. It may not make up for the past two days since I had arrived, but at least it was good to have a few hours together without the guys. I didn't tell her I was still full from lunch with Blake, but I will eat something anyway. That way I wouldn't offend her when she offers to pay for the dinner.

There's a tornado watch by the time we enter this Italian restaurant we decided to eat at. Mum tells me not to worry too much. It was only a watch where a tornado could potentially form, and to take precaution just in case.

I glance outside the window where our table was, looking out onto the main street of Wiley. The sunset turns the sky a shade of orange, red and pink where the clouds are building up. From the dark grey, it looks as if it may rain soon. It didn't look like there will be a storm.

Mum may have told me not to worry too much about the tornado watch, not until a warning is issue, a sickening feeling in my stomach tells me something bad is going to happen. If I tell Mum about the feeling, she may wave off my crazy idea. She will say it's just my fear talking. Maybe it is. Maybe nothing bad will happen, and the whole thing is in my head. A lot of the time when I do start feeling nausea, even if it does mean I'm worried, most of the time no one is concern about a storm approaching. Hopefully we won't stay out for too long and get back to the motel for a shelter if the warnings start becoming frequent throughout the night.

"Charli, try and not worry about the weather, okay?" Mum says with a smile. "Let's enjoy our dinner once our order arrives."

I nod, turning from the window and face her. "I'm just cautious when it comes to storms now. Ever since what happened while we were on holidays, I keep wondering what if a tornado formed. I don't want to ever have to go through that experience again."

"I understand." She gives me a small smile. "It's okay, Charli. You aren't going to go through the same thing again. Try not to worry too much about the weather. We will be safe if a tornado does occur."

"Yeah, maybe we are safe during the day, but if it occurs at night, how do we know if it's on the ground?"

Mum takes a sip of her water. "It's tricky, I know." She places the glass down, licking her lips. "At night you can't see it at all unless it's a stormy night and the lightning may help you to see the outline of the funnel. If there is no storm, power flashes is what tells you that there is one on the ground."

I nod, and then glance out of the window again.

"I spoke to Tommy, Charli," she continues on. "I told him we will continue chasing this week, but then I want to spend the final week of your stay with you."

I turn to face her. "Really?"

"Yes. I realise I haven't acted like a mother to you in the last few years since studying meteorology, and I'm sorry, Charli. With you being here I really hope we have a second chance of being a mother and daughter again." She gives me a small hopeful smile.

I return the smile. "Mum, no matter what happens between us, even if I turn completely against you, we will always be mother and daughter."

Mum's smile grew bigger. Yes, she may have become a workaholic and abandoned Dad and me, acting like we were never a part of her life, but she was still my mother. Even if I do turn against her for abandoning me for her career, I will still always have a small hope inside me that we will become close again. I can't say if I will ever go storm chasing with her again, but I do want to be able to talk to her like we used to before she moved away. Especially things I could never speak to Dad about. Even with the time difference I'm sure we could work something out. I could move here, but there was no way I could leave Dad behind. Or move to Tornado Alley.

"So, how are you finding the trip?" Mum asks. "I know it may not be what you had in mind, and I know the chases haven't gone well because of your fear."

I shrug. "I don't know. It's something I haven't been enjoying at all. Maybe it's something you enjoy, but it's not my idea of fun."

Mum nods. "I understand, Charli."

The waitress comes to our table, placing the pepperoni pizza we had ordered to share in the centre of the table. We thank her and she walks away. We reach for a slice.

"Blake wants me to get into the chase and enjoy it more," I say. "He reckons the chase could expose myself to storms, and help to conquer my fear." I take a bite of the pizza.

"He is right. It will. It might take time, but once you control that fear, you will be fine."

"I have been to a lot of therapy to help with the phobia, but none of them helped."

"I'm sure when you're good and ready, your phobia of storms will someday disappear. It may take time, but eventually you will get over it. Some phobias take longer to get over."

"Yeah," I reply softly.

We carry on eating, moving away from phobias and storm chasing, talking about what we have been up to for the past three years. It felt good to be alone with Mum, talking like we had always done when we used to be close. Though we haven't talked in years and had drifted a part, the closeness seems to be still there. We just had to push our issues aside and put it in the past.

I almost didn't want to leave the restaurant. I wanted to stay here and continuing talking to Mum, knowing we probably wouldn't have any of these conversations around Tommy and Blake. Once we get back to the motel, the only conversations we would be having will be about storms or where we were headed next.

As we pull back into the parking lot of the motel, the sirens blare loudly.

Chapter 11

I cover my ears, squeezing my eyes shut as I tried to block the siren out of my ears. Mum places a hand on my shoulder, telling me everything was alright, but her words couldn't convince me at all.

The siren doesn't stop blaring. Mum tells me we need to get out of the car to seek shelter inside the motel, but I'm frozen in the seat. I begin to cry, begging for the noise to stop.

I hear the car door open then close, knowing Mum had just gotten out, leaving me here. Even when the sirens do stop blaring, I stay in the same position I'm in with my hands still covering my ears.

Soon I hear the passenger door opening beside me.

"Charli, you need to get out of the car," I hear Tommy's voice say to me.

I shake my head. "I can't. I just can't."

He grabs my wrists, pulling my hands away from my ears. He tells me to open my eyes and look at him. I didn't at first, but when he says it the second time, I obey him. I look at him where he is tilting his head, making strong eye contact with me. To see him concern surprised me. He never acted concern towards me when we first met. He was more worried about me interfering with the chase or putting everyone in danger. I have no idea if he still thinks that now. Mixed with the concern look in his eyes was fear. Fear about the tornado that could be approaching us. We were out in the open. A car was not the best shelter for a tornado. Surviving in a vehicle would be a fluke, maybe one percent chance.

"Charli, listen to me," he says. "I know you are scared. I'm scared too. But right now it's not time to freak out and allow your fear to get the better of you. We need to get to safety in case the tornado does come our way. It may miss us. We are going to go to the motel lobby and hide out there until it's safe to go back to our rooms. Can you unbuckle your seat belt for me?"

My body shakes at the very thought of taking shelter in the motel lobby. I recall my very first encounter with a tornado as I held onto my dear life with my parents as the EF2 tornado ripped through the hotel we had stayed at. No. I couldn't take shelter in there. I do not want to relive the nightmare. I want it to end.

Still frozen in fear, I allowed Tommy to take my hand, and lead me out of the car. It's windy, but not strong. Tommy tightens his grip around my wrist so I won't think about letting go. We run across the pavement over to the lobby where everyone staying at the motel was gathering. Mum waits for me at the front and wraps me into a hug as soon as we reach her.

"Where is Blake?" Tommy asks.

"I told him to head inside," Mum answers.

We head inside, finding Blake amongst the crowded room. There are only ten guests staying at the motel tonight, which is good because it would have been disastrous if there was more. The lobby was small and the motel manager with a thick Canadian accent gets us to hide behind the front desk that way we were away from the windows and the front door.

I sit down beside Blake, resting my back up against a cupboard. The knob on the doors behind me stabs my back, and it was hard to move while everyone was cramp into a small place. To my left is Mum while Tommy sits on the other side of Blake. In Blake's lap he had his laptop bag and was holding onto his video camera, filming everything.

Also in the cramp space behind the desk is a mother and father with their two young children who looks to be between the ages four and six years. Another was a young couple in their early to mid-twenties. The motel manager turns on the radio to keep us updated with what is going on outside.

Everyone sits quietly as we listen to the winds, listening for any freight train, whooping and howling sounds to tell us that the tornado was heading our way. So far the winds weren't strong, and I was thankful. I don't want a repeat of the experience from the holiday. Maybe the siren is a false alarm and there was never a tornado.

I watch the children for a second, a boy and girl. At the current moment they were confused with what was happening and was unaware of why we were gathered in the lobby. Both were dressed in their pyjamas and were probably getting ready for bed when the sirens went off. Their parents explain to them calmly with what was happening. The girl sucks on her thumb, cuddling up to her mother, saying she was scared. Her brother tells her not to worry and that he will protect her. I smile at what he said, which reminded me of what Blake had said about protecting me.

I turn back to Blake as he continues to film. Mum sits there quietly, squeezing my hand tightly. Not sure why, I place my other free hand on Blake's knee and let it rest there. I don't look at Blake, but I know he is staring at me. A few seconds later I feel his hand on top of mine. I smile and look up at him, our eyes meeting. He returns the smile.

***

Fifteen minutes passes before the tornado warning is cancel. The radio says that a small tornado had hit the northern part of the town. The motel manager allows us to go back to our rooms, and tells us if there is ever another warning during the night to head down to the front desk or if we couldn't, take shelter in the bathroom. The thought of another warning during the night made me not want to sleep at all.

Mum walks closely beside me, her arm wrapped around me as we walk back to our room. We don't say a word about tonight with what happened in the car earlier. Once we reach our room we say goodnight and head to bed. Mum said we need to get up early again tomorrow.

While Mum drifts off to sleep, snoring softly, I lay there thinking, afraid to fall asleep in case another tornado came. I don't hear the wind at all.

Rain patters down just after midnight. I lay there in bed listening to it until eventually sleep wins, my eyes closing, making me instantly forget about my worries.

Chapter 12

When my parents first made me see a therapist to help with my fear right after the disastrous vacation, one of the things Doctor Henson and I would talk about were dreams. I tell him about the nightmares I would get about the tornado, and how I narrowly miss death as it struck the hotel. Each dream was different every time. Sometimes it was about me huddling up in the lobby with my parents, sometimes Mum would slip away or I am the one who loses grip of my parents as I'm being thrown in the air. In other dreams I am in the car with Dad as the tornado chases us. Or the twister is heading straight towards me, but never really reaches me. Sometimes it passes over my home but surprisingly doesn't damage it, only taking something that truly means something to me like my car or my computer.

Even with all of these dreams, Doctor Henson reckons dreaming about tornadoes could mean anything, and not just on the encounter I have had. He explains there are three possible meanings to why I was seeing these storms in my dreams. The first one could mean of the following emotions: rage, tantrums, confusion of feelings, and other emotions that could make me feel powerless, maybe even experiencing an unstable relationship or situation.

Another reason could mean there is a destructive situation, feeling a lack of control, as well as experiencing disappointments or other complications within my life.

The last meaning could be changes in my life.

At first when he told me all of this, I thought he was crazy and had no idea what he was talking about. Now when I think about it, he is right. For the past seven years a lot of things have changed in my life. My family drifting apart with Mum's big career change, my parents' divorce, anger and confusion with my relationship with Mum, as well as dealing with teenage girls stuff. I still often have dreams about that day. Other dreams represent whatever is happening in my life.

Tonight it's a dream about me being in the hotel lobby with my parents. Mum's grip is tight on my arm, but the winds pull on her, forcing her to let go of me as the winds drag her across the marble floor before lifting her up in the air, throwing her like she is a ragdoll. I scream, but it's drowned out by the howling winds as it destroys everything in its path.

My screams are soon replaced by my mother's soothing voice, as she wakes me from the nightmare. My face is wet with tears, shaken up. Mum sits me up straight and then pulls me into her arms. I press the side of my face against her chest, wetting her shirt with my tears. I immediately calm down as she rubs a hand gently up and down my back, rocking me gently to comfort me.

"Shh, it's okay, Charli," she says in a soothing voice. "It's only a nightmare."

I close my eyes, remembering how she used to comfort me as a young girl from horrible dreams, or when I used to believe that a monster lived in my closet when I was only four years old. Every time I heard a noise outside I thought it was the monster coming to get me. Mum would stay with me until I fall asleep again, assuring me no monster will come get me, and it was all a figment of my imagination.

We sit there in silence in each other's arms, listening to the rain patter down outside.

"Mum, do you ever think about that day when the tornado hit the hotel?" I ask.

Mum strokes my hair. She nods. "Yes, I think about it all the time. I think about how lucky I still have you and your father. I wouldn't know what I would do if I had lost you both."

I think about what Blake had told me earlier today about the real reason why my mother decided to study meteorology. It's something I never really discuss with my mother before, and I wonder if now was the right time to discuss it.

"Blake told me the real reason why you decided to study meteorology," I say.

Mum pulls away from me, stares at me as if she was suddenly caught out doing something she wasn't supposed to be doing. I wait for her to answer me, but she doesn't say a word. As much as I never wanted to believe Blake, I knew he was telling the truth about Mum when she remains silent. I suddenly feel nausea for an unknown reason, not sure if it was because of the dream or the fact that I feel like a horrible daughter for never knowing the truth about my mother. It's something I know I shouldn't feel bad about, especially when she was the one keeping the secret from me, but at the same time I felt like it was something I should have already known about her without ever asking.

"Why didn't you ever tell me the truth?" I ask. "Or even tell Dad?"

Mum remains silent and I figure she was going to ignore me like she has always done. But surprisingly she doesn't. She tells me what Blake had told me. She apologised for never telling Dad and I the truth, afraid Dad would stop her or he wouldn't allow her to pursue her passion for storm chasing. When she chose to do an internship in the United States, she originally didn't want to leave Dad and me. She wanted us to move to the States with her so she was able to continue with research. She was torn when Dad and I declined her offer to move to Tornado Alley.

She pauses. I wait for her to continue on, wanting to know her reasons for choosing to leave Dad and me in the end. Why didn't she just forget about the internship and stayed with us? But she doesn't say anything. She sits there, deep in thought.

When she doesn't say anything at all, I ask her for the answer.

Mum rubs her eyes, weary. "Let's get back to sleep, Charli. We have to get up early."

Mum moves away from me. She is about to turn off the lamp beside her bed when I stop her.

"Mum, please answer my question."

She nods. "Charli, I... I felt distant from your father, so I made the decision to leave him. I know you already hate me for making the decision or even understand why I made it. When I was out here with my colleagues, I felt that this was the place I truly belong."

We stare at each other for a few minutes without saying anything. Mum is the first to break the gaze, switching off the lamp and then lying back down to sleep.

I sit there for a moment in the darkness before lying down, staring up at the ceiling, listening to the rain patter down on the roof. I take a few deep breaths so I wouldn't scream at my mother. Now wasn't the time for us to argue. I still wanted to know the reasons why she chose to leave Dad and me. Even if she said she left Dad because she felt distant, I didn't think it was a good enough excuse to just leave. Maybe I didn't fully understand my parents' relationship, but I still didn't think it was a great excuse to go. There was still an opportunity to work things out with each other.

Maybe there was something else she wasn't telling me. Why? Didn't she think I would understand? I'm nineteen years old next month. I will be able to handle the truth. I'm sure Dad knows the truth too, and he has never told me the real answer either. It was something he never really liked to discuss, which I understand. But as their daughter, I wanted to know what really happened between them. I have the right to know, don't I?

I eventually fall asleep, and when Mum wakes me at the crack of dawn, I regretted every moment not getting enough sleep last night.

Forcing myself out of bed, I get ready. While Mum dresses in the bathroom, I check the radar on her laptop. There were two different storm systems forming, one over northern Texas and another over western Kansas. We wouldn't be able to follow both so I wonder which one we will be chasing today.

We find a diner that is open for breakfast and order our food. Blake and I sit together across from Mum and Tommy. We eat as they stare at the screen of Mum's laptop, studying the radar and discussing which supercell had the best chance of producing a tornado.

After discussing the storm for about twenty minutes, Mum and Tommy settles on the Texas storm, which Mum reckons will be our best chance of seeing a tornado. Not sure how she thinks it will be our best chance, but she spoke in weather terms to explain why that I didn't really understand. We were headed for a place call Prairie Plains, which is approximately an eight hour drive. It was the perfect chance for me to catch up on sleep from last night.

Chapter 13

Mum pulls into the service station to fill up the SUV before continuing on with the chase. We were five minutes away from the small town of Prairie Plains. The clouds were a dark shade of grey, almost black that it made it look like it was dusk when it was only three in the afternoon. White patches of clouds also appear among the dark ones. The thunder rumbles loudly, and it starts to sprinkle. It won't be long until it will be pouring.

Tommy gets out to fill the tank while Mum disappears inside to pay for the petrol.

"Do you want to get out and stretch your legs?" Blake asks me. "We can check out the storm."

I feel the nausea building up in the pit of my stomach. "No thank you."

"Come on. Just take my hand and you will be fine. We won't stand out in the open. We will stand under the shelter, okay?"

I nod. I unbuckle my seat belt and scoot across the backseat to get out Blake's side. He takes my hand and pulls me out. I squeeze his hand tightly as thunder rumbles loudly. In my mind I scream at myself to get back inside to hide from the storm, but my body refuses to listen as it stands beside Blake. We stand near the hood of the car, not going any further than that.

I look around me as the rain comes down heavy. Other storm chasers also pull in to fill up before resuming their chase. Tommy calls out to someone he knows.

We stand there watching the lightning rip across the sky. I was tempted to escape back inside the car, but Blake has a firm grip on my wrist so I couldn't run. My heart beats fast; my head spins as I tried to figure out what to do. Every time I try to pull back from Blake, he grips harder. I couldn't stand here and watch the storm like he wanted me to.

Before I get the chance to beg Blake to allow me to get back in the car, the siren goes off. My heart beats fast, faster than what it did while I was standing here watching the storm with Blake. I suddenly find myself unable to breathe, my chest tightening. I'm not having a heart attack, am I? By the way my heart was beating fast; I wouldn't be surprised if I did have one. Blake loosens his grip on my wrist, turning to me as he asks if I'm alright, but I can't answer him. My mind goes blank as I shut his voice out of my head. All I can think about is getting to safety. I have no idea if a tornado has touched ground yet, but if the warning siren is going off so there has to be something heading our way. Or maybe it was still forming, and everyone was issued to get to safety before it reaches the ground. I don't care where I seek shelter, just as long as I'm safe from the tornado. I need to get Blake, Mum and Tommy to safety. I don't care if they want to chase it. We just can't be out in the open chasing this deadly column of rotating air.

I turn to Blake, my voice shaking as I tell him we needed to take shelter fast. I look around for Tommy who was finishing filling up the car. I couldn't see Mum. Where was Mum? She must be still inside the building. I look around at the other people at the service station. I see them standing around, unsure if they should seek shelter here or to get in their cars to escape. There was no visual on the tornado yet so in the meantime we're safe, but for how long? The other storm chasers scramble to get back into their cars as they quickly pay for their petrol so they could continue their chase.

Blake grabs my arms and makes an attempt to calm me down, but his words fail to comfort me.

Tommy runs over to us. "Blake, get her in the car. I will go get April."

Tommy turns to run inside. Rather than Blake pulling me into the SUV, it was me who pulled him. I shake uncontrollably in the backseat as he tries to calm me down.

"Charli, listen to me," he says, grabbing a hold of my shoulders. "Everything will be alright."

I shake my head. "No, we aren't. A tornado is coming."

"Yes, but it can be anywhere right now. It may not have formed yet. Maybe a funnel cloud has been spotted and they sent out a warning early so people can get to safety."

"Blake, please. Don't make me do this." I burst into tears, instantly blurring my vision. "I know you want to help me to get over my fear, but I really cannot do this. Don't make me chase this storm with you. Please, Blake."

He wipes the tears away from my eyes so I'm able to see again. He stares back at me, worried. He seemed more concerned about me then about the tornado that could be heading our way. I wanted him to stay focus on our safety, not being concerned about me and my phobia. That was the least of my problems right now. Seeking shelter was way more important. "Charli, listen to me. You can do this. Just take a deep breath and breathe. I'm right here. I won't let anything happen to you."

"You can't promise me that anything will happen."

"Maybe I can't promise you that, but I just know we will be fine. Tommy and April will not let anything happen to us."

I shake my head. "No. I can't do this anymore, Blake."

Blake glances over my shoulder. I follow his gaze to see what he was staring at, but before I could actually turn around to see, he cups his hands around my jaw, making me look at him and leans in to kiss me. It was a quick kiss, so quick that I barely had the time to react. He pulls away, leaving my head spin, instantly making me forget what's going on around me and the panic attack I was having. The kiss leaves a tingling feeling on my lips, making me crave for more of him. We stare at each other, shock by what happened between us. I had no idea what to think, and as I stared back at him, I tried to read his facial expression, wondering what he must be going through his mind. I wait for him to kiss me again, but he quickly moves away from me and puts on his seat belt as Mum and Tommy gets into the car.

I continue to sit there staring at him, my heart crushing as Blake sits there like the kiss never happened. He picks up his camera bag from the floor and takes out the camera.

From the corner of my eye I see Mum look my way just as Tommy starts up the car. "Charli, are you alright?"

I nod, but I don't move.

"Okay, well please put on your seat belt," she continues on.

I listen to her and quickly scooted over just as Tommy steps on the accelerator. I put on my belt just as Tommy turns onto the road. Behind us the other storm chasers pull out from the service station, heading in the same direction as us. Mum and Tommy discuss which way we are heading while I stare out the window, smiling as I touch my finger tips to my lips, still feeling Blake's lips on mine.

I turn away from the window and look at Blake, wondering if he too was thinking about the kiss. He glances my way just as our eyes meet, making my heart skip a beat. He gives me a small smile and then turns back to his camera.

Whether Blake likes me or not, the panic attack I had a few minutes ago has disappeared. And I'm glad Blake had kissed me to keep my mind off the storm. Though I wasn't sure for how long it will last until we find the tornado that is storm warned.

Chapter 14

I notice a tint of green in the clouds as Tommy drives through the small town of Prairie Plains. So far there has been no sign of a tornado on the ground, just a developing wall cloud forming on the outskirts of the town over a field.

I should be having a panic attack right now, but the storm wasn't on my mind. All I could think about was the kiss Blake and I shared. It was the one thing keeping me distracted.

But I soon had to snap myself back to reality when Tommy pulls over on the side of the road near a field outside of town. Other storm chasers drive past us as they sit themselves at different locations to get the best view of the storm. Both Mum and Tommy get out of the car to observe the clouds. Blake and I remain in the car, sitting there in silence, unsure if we should get out or say something to each other.

"Are you coming out to look?" he asks me.

I shrug.

"You should. Come on."

He opens the door and hops out, leaving me alone in the car. I take a deep breath, telling myself I can do this, and step outside. A cool breeze hits me and I instantly start feeling nausea as I caught sight of the wall cloud forming across the field to the west of us. A funnel cloud has already started to form. It won't be long until it's on the ground.

I can do this, I tell myself, taking in a deep breath and exhaling it slowly. *There is nothing to worry about.*

Someone's hand rests on my right shoulder. The feel of Blake's hand immediately comforts me. I turn to face him. My heart sinks with disappointment when he isn't looking at me directly, but out in the field where he films the forming funnel. I follow his gaze, trying not to freak out as lightning rips through the sky, thunder following shortly after. I bite down on my lip to fight back tears.

I remove Blake's hand from my shoulder and hold on it, squeezing it tightly as he holds onto his camera with one hand. The funnel is almost on the ground, and soon we will be seeing a debris cloud. Mum suggests we head up north. Getting back into the car, we head in that direction.

I stare out the window as Tommy drives, watching the funnel cloud and trying to keep calm as much as possible. Taking deep breaths don't help me to stay calm, and I can already feel another panic attack coming on. To avoid another one, I think about the kiss, biting my lip as I let the smile spread across my face.

The kiss distracts me for a short time until Blake shouts out excitedly that the tornado was now on the ground. I turn my attention to the funnel ripping up the field, debris flying around it. I spot a farm a couple of miles ahead and prayed silently to myself that the residents there were safe underground. Even though we were a safe distance from the twister, I still felt unsafe being inside this car and I wasn't sure how I could restrain myself any longer without freaking out. Although my window was closed, Tommy's driver side window wasn't. The feel of the wind on my skin sent my heart beating rapidly. To help comfort me a little, I hold onto the door handle tightly, my knuckles turning white.

"Charli, I need you to do a favour for me," Blake says. "I can't get a good shot from here. Could you please take the camera and film the tornado for me?"

The very first thought I had when he asked me to film the tornado is how could he trust me with the camera? I would be shaking uncontrollably. I wouldn't be able to get a steady shot for him.

I take the camera from him and pointed the lens at the window. The raindrops slid down the glass, not giving me much of a great view. Blake suggests I wind down the window. At first I was unsure about winding it down, terrified that I would be suck out of it and being thrown in the air like a paper plane.

I quickly push the fear out of my head and push the button on the door to wind down the window. I was thankful my hair was tied back into a ponytail as the winds ripped through the car. The wind roars. For a moment I think I may have stopped breathing as I suddenly feel faint, like I would pass out at any second.

"April, is there a road we are able to drive onto that could allow us to intercept?" Tommy asks.

"There should be a road coming up to our left soon just after this farm," Mum informs him.

Biting my lip, I look through the lens of the camera as the tornado rips through a barn. It sounded like a freight train was passing by. I almost let out a squeal, and quickly clap a hand over my mouth. As much as I was terrified and didn't want to be here, I had to force myself to realise that the others do want to be here. Blake had explained to me yesterday about how important this was for my mother to collect as much data she needs for each chase, even if this chase wasn't important to me. Having a panic attack right now may make her lose focus, and could potentially put us all in danger if any wrong decision is made. She may even end it, and I knew none of them will like it if I ruin the whole chase.

Excitement rises in Mum's and Tommy's voices as the vortex moves across the plains. Blake scoots across the backseat until he was behind me. He places his hands on my arms to stop them from shaking so the camera wouldn't move around as much.

Tommy speeds as fast as he could, overtaking two cars in front of him and quickly changing back in the right lane before he collided with oncoming traffic. Some vehicles were parked on the side of the road waiting for the tornado to pass or to film and take photographs. Others quickly zoom by to get away from the tornado.

Blake stays close to me as Tommy manages to pass the tornado, and turns left sharply at the intersection Mum had told him about. The tyres screech as we turned in a hurry. Blake quickly grabs his camera from my hand before I drop it out the window. I was thankful the window was down, otherwise I would have smashed my face against the glass as Blake and I jerk forward. Blake's body crushes me up against the door. He apologises and then moves away from me as soon as Tommy drives straight.

The tornado is now coming at us from the side. Mum wanted Tommy to pull over the side so she could put a probe in its path, but Tommy declines the idea. Within sixty seconds or less the tornado will be on top of us. Tommy pulls to the side, staying clear of the danger zone so we wouldn't get suck up. He backs up a little as debris heads our way.

Knowing I would scream, Blake claps a hand over my mouth as he holds onto his camera. We sit there watching as the tornado cross the road in front of us, debris surrounding the base. I try to look away, but it wasn't easy to turn my head when Blake was holding onto me. The wind roars and howls as the funnel crosses the road, making it sound like a monster.

As soon as it passes us into the next field, Blake lets go of me, quickly moving to the other side, winding down his window and keeps his camera on the vortex.

"Is there a road that turns right up here or do we have to turn back on the other road?" Tommy asks Mum.

"No, there is no right turn up here," Mum says, looking at a map on her computer. "Make a U-turn and go back to the road we were on before."

Tommy does a U-turn and then step on the accelerator, speeding off to the road we were on earlier to catch up with the twister.

Blake moves to my side of the vehicle again so he could film the funnel I lean back against the seat so he could make the shot.

"Blake, get back in your seat and put on your seat belt," Mum warns him.

"I need to make this shot, April."

"I know, but I need you to sit back. I don't want you to be flying through the windscreen if we have to stop in a hurry."

Blake listens and sits back in his seat, putting on his seat belt. He then gives me the camera, asking me to film again. I take the camera, shaking.

"Is there a way we can get ahead of the tornado?" Mum asks Tommy.

"I'm not sure," Tommy says with his eyes half on the road and half on the storm. "We could possibly get off this road where there won't be a lot of traffic, then that would be good."

"There is a cross intersection coming up here. Take a left."

Tommy does as he is told. As soon as he reaches the cross intersection, he takes a left. He travels a mile up the road until he was able to take a right, and chases after the tornado. The good thing about being in the open plains was there wasn't much debris for the tornado to suck up or destroy. Thankfully there weren't too many properties around either and I was glad people would be safe from this monstrous whirlwind. Hopefully people in their cars will be safe. There weren't many trees either, so we didn't have to worry too much with branches being thrown as missiles at us, and being out in the middle of nowhere there weren't many power lines on every road.

I hand Blake his camera.

"Hey, hey, another funnel is forming just to the east of this tornado!" Blake cries out.

Chapter 15

"There is some rotation in the clouds just to the northwest of us," Tommy points out as he continues to drive. "Looks like a third funnel might drop."

Mum doesn't respond to Tommy. She is too focused on the tornado Blake had spotted forming to our east. Tommy keeps his eyes on the road, following the other tornado, searching for the best possible way to intercept. I wasn't sure what I was supposed to focus on. My eyes darted everywhere, praying silently to myself that we wouldn't get caught in the storm, especially with the previous incident from yesterday.

"The tornado is on the ground!" Blake cries out excitedly.

I force myself to look through the back window, seeing the white vortex heading towards us. Tommy gains speed to get ahead. I forget about the other one that is ahead of us, and watch the new tornado on the ground. I bite my lip to prevent me from screaming and hold onto my seat belt as tightly as I could.

"Tommy, turn right at this road up ahead, and pull over," Mum says just as the first tornado crosses the road she wants to go on. "Let me get out here and drop the probe."

"Are you sure?" Tommy double checks her decision.

"Yes, let me out here."

"Alright. You get out. I will stay in the car in case we have to escape in a hurry."

Mum looks over her shoulder at me as Tommy turns right on the road. "Charli, I need you to help me with the probe."

Before I could protest, Mum jumps out of the car as soon as Tommy brakes. Blake jumps out also to film the tornado coming at us. I feel the power of the wind as it whips through the car, slamming the car doors that both Mum and Blake left opened shut.

"Charli, get out now!" Tommy yells at me over the wind.

Listening to him, I unbuckle my seat belt and force myself to get out of the car before Tommy or someone else yells at me. As soon as I place my feet on the tar road, almost being blown over by the strong wind, and battered with rain, drenching my clothes, I immediately wanted to get back in the car and seek shelter. But I couldn't seek shelter right now. No matter what my fear was, I had to help my mother so she was able to collect the data she needed for her job.

I hurried over to Mum as she opens up the back boot. Blake kept filming the tornado as it gets closer to us, excitedly saying how great the footage will look on his film.

Mum grabs one end of the probe while I grab the other. Together we lift up the orange probe and carry it quickly to the side of the road.

"Guys, get in the car now!" Tommy yells out to us as he gets out of the car. "The first tornado is backtracking towards us!"

Mum looks over my shoulder and curses.

Two tornadoes were headed towards us, and we had only seconds to get out of the way.

We quickly drop the probe on the side of the road. Mum quickly closes the boot, and then runs to her side of the car. I run, and when I open the door, the wind lifts me up. I grab the door, hanging onto it tightly, screaming at the top of my lungs.

"Charli, hang on!" Blake screams as he scoots across the backseat, grabbing my arm.

Tommy was about to get out to help me, but Mum screams at him to step on it before we are all suck up. Blake hangs on me tightly, pulling me into the car. Mum hangs onto his legs as he too is almost sucked out of the car. Tommy steps on the accelerator, the back tyres screeching as he speeds off down the road. I'm pulled into the car. Blake embraces me tightly as I breathe heavily. My throat is sore from screaming, and my face is wet, unsure if it was from tears or from the rain.

Mum is now pulling me into her arms as Tommy gets to a safe distance, and spins the car around so we are facing the two tornadoes. Mum hugs me tightly.

"Oh my gosh!" Blake says. "This is totally amazing."

He jumps out of the car to film, follow by Tommy. Mum tells me to come out and have a look, but I refuse to. How could they even think about going out there after what had just happened? Mum gives me a disappointing look, like she really wanted me to join her outside, enjoying every single moment of this storm. Seeing the disappointment in her eyes sends my heart sinking deeply in my chest. Even if she wanted me to enjoy this moment, I couldn't feel the same excitement she could feel or the same as the others. She releases me from her embrace and gets out of the car, leaving me behind.

I look up to see the tornadoes meeting in the centre of the road, merging together. Mum jumps up and down excitedly, as the funnel crosses over the probe, talking about amazing data it will collect, and how she has never seen anything like this before.

The now large tornado, almost a mile wide, stalls in the centre of the road. I hid behind the seat so I couldn't see it. How could the others stand out there, not knowing what this storm could do? At any moment the tornado could change direction and head our way.

I peek around the seat just in time to see the tornado changing course. It looks as if it was heading our way. None of the others seem too worried. As I jump out of the car, ready to warn them, I sigh with relief as it shifts to northeast, away from us. Blake continues to follow the funnel with his camera, while Mum cheered happily. Tommy was fairly quiet and wasn't cheering like Mum. I'm sure he was cheering happily in his own way, he just wasn't showing it.

I stand beside Blake.

"This is amazing, isn't it, Charli?" he says excitedly.

I don't answer him as I watch the tornado disappear in the distance. We stand there in silence.

"Thank you for saving me, Blake," I say after a few minutes.

He turns to face me, and smiles. "It's no problem."

I return the smile and then hug him. He then turns his camera off and walks over to Mum and Tommy. As I go to follow him, I stop in my tracks when I see them lip locking. Blake didn't seem to be bothered by them kissing as he strolls over to the probe.

I stand there as the rain started to slow down. I wasn't sure what I was supposed to be feeling when I saw them – confuse, angry or happy. Mum has never mention anything about dating since divorcing Dad, and he has never dated anyone either. He could if he wanted to, but he didn't want to make me feel like he was replacing my mother.

"Mum?"

Mum pulls away from Tommy. He looks at me like he was caught doing something he wasn't supposed to, while Mum looked as if she had made a mistake.

"Charli."

I look from Mum to Tommy and back to her. "Mum, what's going on? Are you... are you and Tommy...?" I choke on the last word.

Tommy and Mum look at each other before turning back to me.

"Yes, your mother and I are together," he replies.

My stomach twists into knots. "For how long?"

"For three years," Mum answers.

Three years. That's how long she and Dad have been divorced for. Now I understand the real reason why she left. It wasn't just because she wanted to stay in America to continue storm chasing, but she wanted to stay because she had met someone else other than Dad.

She had an affair.

She lied to hide her affair.

I wonder if Dad knows about it.

"Is that why you really left, Mum?" I ask. "To be with *him*?" I say the last word like it was poison.

Mum finds it hard to look at me. "Yes and no, Charli."

"What do you mean yes and no?" I raise my voice.

"Can we not do this now, please Charli? We should really get the probe and head to a motel."

I shake my head. "No. You are going to tell me everything now. I'm not going to allow you to leave things the way it is and not tell me at all. I want to know the truth about why you really left."

Mum looks at the ground, biting her lip before looking at me. She tells me she had met Tommy while on her internship. She admitted there was chemistry between them, but she didn't do anything at first, still remaining faithful to Dad. When she asked Dad and me to come live in the United States with her, she felt lonely when we wouldn't join her. That's when she had the affair. In mid-October she had chosen to return home to file divorce so she could be with Tommy.

I take one look at Tommy and had to restrain myself from doing something I know I would regret. How dare he take Mum away from me? Who does he think he is?

Does Blake know they were together? How can he not tell me that they were together?

Without saying a word, I started walking down the road. Mum calls out to me to come back, but I don't turn. Over my shoulder I tell her not to speak to me ever again.

Someone grabs my arm. I spin around to push the hand off me.

"Charli, let's talk about this," Tommy says.

Frowning at him, I shove him in the chest. "Stay away from me. Don't ever come near me again. Don't you dare try to replace my father because you are nothing like him."

"Don't get mad with him, Charli," Mum says, coming up behind him. "Look, I know you're mad at me, but please don't take your anger out on Tommy."

"Oh yeah?" I say. "And exactly when were you planning to tell me the truth, Mum? Does Dad know the real reason why you left him?"

She shakes her head. "No. He knows nothing about the affair and I don't want him to ever know."

I imagine Dad's heart breaking to a million pieces knowing that the woman he had been married to for almost eighteen years leaving him for another man. It wasn't right at all.

Maybe if we never went on that stupid vacation, we wouldn't be in the tornado's path. I wouldn't be terrified of storms, and Mum wouldn't have made the decision to study meteorology.

"I hate you," I tell her. "You don't care about me, so I'm never going to care about you."

I see the hurt in her eyes from my words. I don't feel bad for what I have said at all.

"Charli, you don't mean that," she says, blinking back tears.

"Of course I mean it. I don't care about your stupid job either. I want to leave and go home. And once I leave, I don't ever want to see you again."

"Charli."

"No, Mum. Don't try and beg me to stay, because it's not going to work at all. I'm leaving on the next flight home. Now take me to the airport or I will walk there."

"Don't be silly, Charli."

"I said take me there this instant!"

Tommy and Mum stares at me, startle by my actions.

When they don't answer me, I turn and continue walking down the road. I hear Mum call after me, but doesn't make an effort to come after me. Someone's footsteps run along the tar road, but I don't look behind me to see who it is.

The person grabs my arm. I spin around to fight them off, finding that it's Blake. He tightens his grip on me.

"Charli, please don't go," he begs.

"Let go of me, Blake."

"No, I'm not letting you go."

"Why?"

"It's because right now is not a great idea to be walking around out in the open during a storm. Another funnel could form or the same tornado could backtrack this way once more. Where are you going to take shelter, Charli?"

He was right, although I doubt another funnel would form or the tornado would backtrack again. It's far in the distance right now, but then again tornadoes are unpredictable.

"You knew all along that Tommy was dating my mother, didn't you?" I say.

Blake shakes his head. "No. I didn't know at all. He never told me anything about dating someone. Your mother and Tommy never really showed any chemistry around me."

I believe him, and I knew there was no reason to be mad at him at all.

"Please, Charli," he pleads. "Come back to the car."

I sigh with frustration. "Fine. I will come, but I'm serious about wanting to leave."

Chapter 16

Tommy didn't drive me to the nearest airport like I had requested. Instead he made a non-stop trip to Brennan Heights, where both Tommy and Mum had decided not to spend the night in a motel, and make the two hour drive home. The trip was silent as no one made a sound, only the radio breaking the sound barrier.

Brennan Heights was a small town, just a couple of miles from the Colorado and Kansas border. It's night when we arrive. Lightning could be seen in the distance and I wonder if the storm will come our way. I hope it doesn't.

Tommy pulls into the driveway of a small house. Mum turns to him, thanking him, promising to call tomorrow. I narrow my eyes at her as I get out of the car. Blake gives me a wave, but I'm not in the mood to wave back to him.

Mum opens the back boot to grab her things. She was about to grab my suitcase, but I grab it before she does. Without saying anything, I head towards the front door, pulling my suitcase behind me. Mum says goodbye to the guys before Tommy backs out of the driveway, disappearing down the street.

I stand at the front door, watching my mother. She turns from the road and looks at me. I can just see the outline of her face from a nearby street light, lighting up the front yard. After a few minutes of staring at each other, she walks over to me with her overnight bag. She digs through her pocket for her keys. She then uses the light from her phone to find the right key. She unlocks the front door and I push pass her to get inside.

The lounge room was small, just a couch, television and bookshelf. Boxes were scattered around the room, labels were written on them to what was inside.

"I'm really sorry about the mess," Mum apologises. "I have boxes everywhere at the moment. I'm getting ready to move at the end of next month. I only have one bedroom so if you want you can sleep in my room and I will take the couch."

"The couch is fine, Mum," I answer, dumping my suitcase next to the couch and then take a seat.

"Sweetie, you're the guest and I think the bed would be much better for you."

I roll my eyes. "Mum, I said the couch is fine. Now, please leave me alone."

Mum slowly nods her head, blinking back the tears that are forming in her eyes. "Okay, you can sleep on the couch. Listen, I'm going to put my stuff away and then we can eat something for dinner. What would you like? I can cook you something or we can order pizza. Or would you prefer Chinese?"

My stomach grumbles at the mention of food. I hadn't eaten anything since lunch. Any kind of food would be great right now, but I didn't want to eat anything in the same room as my mother.

"I'm not hungry," I answer.

"Are you sure? I can fix us something."

"I said I'm not hungry."

Mum nods. "Okay. I'm just going to unpack. If you do feel hungry, you can help yourself to anything you want to eat. If you want to order food, you can."

Without answering, I sat back on the couch and put my feet up like I own it. I pull out my phone. As soon as I put the AirPods in, Mum takes it as a clue to leave. I smile once she is gone.

I wait for a few minutes until I hear my mother's bedroom door close. I then sit up and take out my AirPods. It was no use lying here, pretending to listen when the battery is flat. I place the phone back in my bag. I will worry about charging it later. I reach for the TV remote on the coffee table and switch on the television. I flip through the channels to find the news, hopefully showing the weather. I find a news bulletin issuing a tornado warning across Dante County. I have no idea what county we were in, so I had no idea if I really needed to worry or if I should warn Mum. The weather reporter pointed out where the risk was for the towns that needed to be on alert, but I didn't recognise any of the places. We must be in a safe location away from the storm.

I grab my charger and plug it into my phone, pulling up the weather app. It's slow loading because of the poor internet connection.

I decided not to worry too much. Right now it wasn't raining and there was no storm, except for the faint sound of thunder in the distance. I should be safe here if a tornado does approach.

Leaving the television on about the tornado warning, I walk over to the window and stand beside it, peaking out. I watch the droplets of rain run down the glass. There were no signs of a tornado at all, and everything seemed calm. There was a slight small breeze, but no strong winds.

"What are you up to, Charli?" Mum asks me.

I don't answer her and continue to stare out the window. I wait for her to say something else, but she is silent. I figure maybe she has gone and disappear what she needed to do to keep out of my way. When I turn to look back at her, she is staring at the television, listening carefully to the news bulletin.

She curses and then she leaves the room, entering her own.

I turn back to the street to see Tommy's SUV pulling into the drive way. I narrow my eyes, thinking it's Tommy returning to see Mum. But when Mum walks back into the lounge room, speaking to him on the phone, I realise it wasn't him. I glance back outside to see Blake emerging, running to the front door to escape the rain.

"Do you think there's a chance of the tornado hitting us?" Mum asks Tommy.

I walk over to the door to open it for Blake. His arm was in mid-air where he was just about to knock when I opened it, inviting him inside out of the rain.

"No, I haven't checked the radar." Mum walks to her room.

"There's a tornado warning," I tell Blake.

He nods. "I know. I heard it on the radio on my way here. We need to take precaution tonight. It's not clear whether or not if the tornado will hit us, but we are in Dante County. The report hasn't said anything about it hitting our town, but you just never know what the storm could do."

Mum enters the room with her laptop while still on the phone with Tommy. She sits down on the couch and opens up her computer to check the radar. She curses. "This storm is going to be huge, Tommy."

"I know," Tommy says over the phone. "What are the chances of the storm hitting Brennan Heights? We are just to the east of the storm that is travelling northeast."

"Maybe. Do you know if the manager of the motel you're staying at knows about the warning?"

I turn to look at Blake with a puzzle look. "You guys are staying in a motel? I thought you live in Brennan Heights."

"No, Tommy and I live two towns over in Dale," Blake explains. "Tommy was too tired to drive any further tonight so we decided to spend the night in a motel. So anyway, have you eaten yet?"

"Not yet."

"Would you like to go get something to eat?"

I stare at him like he was crazy. "Blake, there is a tornado warning."

"Yes, I know that," he says, slipping his hands into his pockets.

"I don't think it's wise for us to go out in this weather. We should stay near a shelter just in case. Mum said the tornado could still hit our town."

"It could. Tommy also said that the storm is moving northeast of Brennan Heights. We are just to the east so we should be safe."

I wasn't sure if I wanted to believe Blake. He could be right. The tornado could hit our town. The weather report hasn't put this town in the danger path so we should be right, shouldn't we? We still had to stay alert even if we weren't in the danger zone. Maybe we will be lucky, maybe we won't. Maybe it's all depending on the whole storm itself. I know only so little about these storms. I guess you could say one thing about how the storm could react, but then it can change within a blink of an eye. Whatever does happen with this storm, I hope it doesn't come anywhere near our town. Although Mum is thinking differently about the storm to what they are saying on the weather report, but at the same time I wonder if the things she is saying is even true. She has been lying to me for a while, so I had no idea if what she was saying about the tornado is true.

And even if Mum is wrong about the tornado, I still didn't want to go out to dinner with Blake. Not when there is an approaching thunderstorm. The thunder is getting louder. It won't be long until the storm will be on top of us.

And maybe a possible tornado.

"I will call you back later, Tommy," Mum says. "I'm going to get a few things together before the storm does hit." She hangs up and then looks over at us. "Blake, hey, what are you doing here?"

"I thought I would come over to see if Charli would like to go out for dinner."

Mum shakes her head. "No, not tonight Blake. I think its best you both stay in until this storm passes."

"April, come on. Let me take Charli out for a little while. It will give you some time to unpack, maybe have some time to yourself after the long trip."

"Blake, a tornado warning has been issued within the Dante County."

"Yes, I'm aware of that. But the storm is travelling northeast from here so there is a chance a tornado won't come anywhere near us."

"It doesn't matter, Blake. The storm could change course. Our town is on alert, and even though we aren't exactly in the danger path, we still have a chance of the storm heading our way. Now,

Tommy is going to stay at the motel tonight. If you both are feeling hungry, I will fix you something."

She disappears into the kitchen, opening and closing the pantry cupboards to check what food there was to cook.

Blake turns to me. "Sorry, Charli, but it looks like we're staying here tonight. It might be for the best. It's dark and a tornado is a lot harder to see at night. We don't want to be caught somewhere in it."

Rather than answering Blake, I just stand there, taking in what both Mum and Blake have been saying about this possible tornado. There was a chance this storm could produce one that could head our way or to another town. How do I know who is correct and who isn't? Is there any possible way knowing what this storm could do?

I look around the room, ignoring Mum when she called out to Blake and I if we would like pasta for dinner. Blake answers for me while I study the room, wondering where the best place would be to hide if a tornado does strike. It would all depend on the strength of the cyclone. From what Blake had explained to me when we were at the library back in Wiley, Missouri is that if it's a strong tornado we may be safe inside an interior room of the first floor, while seeking shelter in a basement or storm cellar was mostly best if it was a violent tornado. There was no basement in my mother's home. I wonder if she has a cellar. If not, the bathroom will be our only shelter. Would we be safe in there?

"Do you know if my Mum has a storm cellar?" I ask Blake.

Blake shrugs. "I'm not really sure. I think she does."

I imagine different scenarios of trying to keep ourselves safe in the tornado, but each scenario ended badly. I breathe heavily, unable to think straight as I realise being inside this building wasn't going to keep any of us safe.

"Charli, breathe," Blake says, grabbing my shoulders.

I take deep breathes, but it doesn't relax me at all. Not when I keep thinking about the scenarios.

"Blake, I need to get out of here."

I'm on the ground now, unable to breathe. Memories of the tornadoes I have already been in flooded my mind. Blake is leaning in front of me, trying to calm me down, but his words are dim. I tell him that we aren't safe here in short breathes. Soon Mum is also beside me, trying to get me to calm down. She hands me a glass of water. I gulp it down.

When I calm down, Mum strokes my face, asking if I was okay. I nod.

"If you're worry about the storm, Charli, don't be," she continues on. "It's hard to say whether or not if there will be a tornado."

"What if there will be one?" I ask. "How do we know we will be safe?"

Mum stares at me, thinking about my words. She then gets off the floor and grabs her laptop from the coffee table. She sits down on the couch to take another look at the radar. Blake helps me off the floor and we walk over to the couch, peaking over Mum's shoulder.

"Brennan Heights is to the east of the echo hook that's forming at the end of the cell," Blake points out. "The storm is travelling northeast so we should be safe."

I feel nausea. Even though Blake says we should be safe, it wasn't enough to make me feel better.

Mum continues to stare at the screen, trying to figure out this weather system. "I don't know about this storm. Even if it looks like we are away from the danger path, the winds could change and the storm could head our way."

"I'm sure we will be fine, April," Blake says. "Listen, I will take good care of Charli. I will make sure we are close to a shelter."

Mum looks up at us. "It's not the shelter I'm worried about you guys finding. Maybe if it was during the day I would, but's it's night. I'm worried if the tornado does cross your path, you won't see it coming towards you."

Blake nods. "I understand."

Mum closes the laptop. "Okay, I will let you go out, but I want you to be careful. Blake, since you have more experience with tornadoes than Charli, I need you to look out. If you think the storm is getting worse, find shelter. Don't be out on the street. Call me if anything happens."

Blake promises and then takes my hand, leading me out the door. The rain is starting to get heavy as we step outside, quickly running to the car. I almost scream when a flash of lightning rips through the sky. Blake unlocks the car just as the thunder sounds, and I quickly dive into the front seat, slipping on my seat belt and then hang onto the door handle tightly that my knuckles turn white.

"Are you alright?" Blake asks me, slipping on his seat belt.

I turn to look at him. "Are you sure we should be going out in this storm? Shouldn't we wait until it's over?"

Blake takes my hand and squeezes it. "Try and not worry too much, okay? Think about how we are going to enjoy a nice evening with each other." He starts the engine and backs out of the driveway.

I smile at the thought, making me think of the kiss earlier. "So where are we going?"

"There is this awesome Mexican place on the main street of Brennan Heights. You will love it."

"Does it have a storm shelter?"

Blake smiles and shakes his head. "You really do not stop thinking about storms, do you?"

"I just want to be safe."

"I know. No, the restaurant doesn't have a storm shelter, but if anything happens we will take cover in the bathroom."

It wasn't something I felt satisfied with when sheltering from the tornado, but I guess it was good enough even though it didn't make me feel safe at all. I wanted to argue with Blake about where I really wanted to go so I do feel secure, but I didn't want to ruin this evening with him. Not after what happened this afternoon with Mum and Tommy.

I look out the window, watching the clouds as lightning rips through the sky. The car's engine drowns out the thunder as we travel along the road. I watch the trees as they sway in the gentle breeze, looking for any signs of a tornado. So far there weren't any signs of one. There were no power flashes, only lightning from the storm.

I keep in mind we will be safe.

Chapter 17

The rain comes down heavier once we reach the restaurant. I didn't want to get out of the car, but Blake drags me out and we make a dash for shelter. We were completely drenched by the time we get inside.

A waitress greets us and leads us to a table. The restaurant is full tonight, and I was surprise it was considering Brennan Heights was a small town. It felt like everyone in the town was here. We were lucky enough to get a table. Unfortunately, it was right near the window. I would feel a lot safer in a booth that's in the far corner, away from the window so I didn't have to glance outside at the storm. Thankfully the Mexican music that's playing in the restaurant is drowning out the sound of the thunder rumbling.

The waitress hands us our menus and then steps away, promising to return in a few minutes.

I stare at the menu, unsure what I wanted to order.

"So do you come to this place often?" I ask Blake.

"Sometimes."

"What's your recommendation on the menu?"

"The nacho cheese is my favourite. It's the one meal I always order when I come here. This place makes the best nacho cheese."

"Well then, I will try it out."

I glance down at the menu to see what drinks were available.

"So what's going to happen with you and your mom?" Blake asks.

I shrug, putting down the menu. "I don't know. I'm going to see if I can leave tomorrow. I'm glad you ask me out to dinner. I couldn't stand to stay in that house with her."

"Can't you stay a little longer? It has only been three days."

"I know, but in the last three days I realise my mother and I have drifted apart so much that I doubt our relationship will ever be fix."

"What your mother and you need to do is work things out, and sort out what caused you to drift apart."

Before I could answer him, the lights begin to flicker. We sit there quietly, watching the lights. Most people in the restaurant carried on with their dinner, acting like the beams were none of their concern, while some were wondering what was wrong with them. Some small kids mumble to their parents that they were scared.

After a few minutes the room falls into darkness, along with the music cutting off. People scream from the sudden darkness and the small children begin to cry.

I look at Blake, only just able to see the outline of his figure. A flash of lightning brightens up the restaurant for a brief second before returning to darkness. Blake is staring out the window. Thunder rumbles loudly, making the window beside me rattle from the vibration. I had to bite my lip from screaming, and grab the edge of the table tightly to resist myself from crawling under the table to hide.

I glance outside also, seeing the whole street in darkness. Behind me some people were starting to leave since there was no use in staying here if there was a blackout.

Blake's phone rings and he quickly answers it. I can hear Tommy's panicking voice on the other end, which keeps cutting out over the static.

"Where... you?" Tommy says.

"What? I can't hear you, Tommy," Blake says. "You are breaking up."

"Get...shelter... Tornado... ground."

Tommy's voice cuts out and all we can hear is a dialling sound.

A nauseous feeling forms in the pit of my stomach.

This isn't good.

"What is he saying, Blake?" I ask.

"I think he was asking us where we are and told us to take shelter. There is a tornado on the ground."

"Tornado? But the siren hasn't gone off."

"Sometimes there is no warning at all. Since it's night, it's a lot harder to spot. Maybe the siren has gone off, but we were unable to hear it because of the loud music in here."

"So what are we going to do?"

"I don't know."

He watches the people that are walking out of the restaurant as the manager is telling us to leave, apologising for the unexpected blackout. My stomach twists into knots, which makes the nausea worse, my heart beating fast. This blackout isn't caused by the thunderstorm at all. It's probably caused by down power lines.

A tornado is coming.

Mum is right. The storm did change course and is now heading towards this town.

I can't breathe.

Blake quickly rushes to my side, grabbing my hands before I completely break down.

"Hey, we are going to be fine," he tells me.

"The tornado is coming." I blink back the tears.

"I know, and we will stay here and keep safe from the storm."

I look behind me and see the families leaving the restaurant, unaware they were stepping out into danger.

"Blake, we need to stop these people from going outside," I say as I turn back to him.

Blake looks over at the people leaving. He then grabs my hand; dragging me to the entrance and pushing pass everyone.

"Wait!" he shouts. "We can't go outside. A tornado is heading our way."

"Are you sure?" a man with glasses asks. "The siren hasn't gone off."

Just as the man mentions it, the siren blares loudly. No one moves, glancing around as to figure out where the tornado could be coming from, and where we should take shelter.

Squeezing Blake's hand tightly, I look outside to see if there was any sign of a tornado approaching us. My heart beats fast as I can see the wind picking up outside, follow by lightning and then thunder clapping loudly. It was so dark outside that I still wonder how we were meant to see the tornado coming.

The manager of the restaurant starts moving us to the centre of the restaurant, away from the windows, and telling us to take shelter in the restrooms. As I look around at all the customers and staff members, I wonder how we are all going to fit in there, estimating that there were at least thirty people, maybe more of us.

We make our way to the restrooms. Something hits the roof just as we begin to move. I squeeze Blake's hand tighter. The next minute one of the front windows shatters, pieces of glass flying everywhere. A flash of lightning shows a piece of wood flying through the room. We are back in darkness before we know where it went. Hopefully it hasn't hit anyone. Some people scream, while the children cry. Thunder follows shortly after, but the rumbling sound doesn't stop. It sounded as if a freight train was going by. The restaurant was right near the railway. But by the sickening feeling in my stomach, there is not train going pass.

Another flash of lightning rips across the sky, revealing the debris being picked up from the building across the street. Difficult to see in the complete darkness with only a second to see it as the lightning brightens up the sky, revealing the large vortex heading our way.

I squeal Blake's name. He sees the funnel. He then shouts out to everyone to hurry. We only have seconds to get to shelter before this place will be ripped to shreds.

More debris is being thrown through the building, causing everyone to panic as they run and shove other people out of the way. The darkness doesn't make it any easy for us to see where we are going. I almost trip over when someone bumps into me, but lucky Blake was hanging onto my wrist tightly.

We make it into the bathroom. Blake drags me into a stall. It wasn't easy seeing everyone in the room as we all crouch down and cramp together. I think someone was in the stall with us, but I couldn't see them. Blake closes the door in the stall and locks it. He then crouches down beside me, staying close to me. To hang onto something, he tells me to hold onto the wooden pole holding up the stalls. I listen to him, even though I know holding onto it was going to be pointless. The wind was going to rip this stall right out of the tile floor. Sitting in the darkness, we hear the smashing and the sound of a freight train, waiting for the tornado to hit us, and praying we all would be alright.

My heart beats fast, and I think I may have stopped breathing. Bile raises, and I quickly swallow it. Right now wasn't a great idea to be sick.

I close my eyes. At the back of my mind I knew Blake and I were going to die. There is no way we are going to be able to survive this large tornado. I think about Dad, wondering if I would ever get to see him again. It would tear his heart to pieces, and he would blame himself for letting me visit Mum.

And then I thought of Mum. I may be mad at her, wishing I have never came here to see her again after three years. Was the three years even worth it? I have only been with her for three days, and now it could possibly be my last. The guilt of the way I have been treating her is now stabbing me in the stomach, making me feel even worse than what I already am. I have acted like a total jerk since arriving here. How can I leave this world knowing the way I have treated her? I think about the last words I had said to her: *What if it was? How do we know we will be safe?* Oh gosh, I never said goodbye to her.

I hope she is alright and is safe from this tornado.

I open my eyes when Blake places an arm around my waist as he huddles closer to me, telling me to hang on tightly as I could.

I nod, my face wet with tears. The smashing, the freight train and howling noise is getting louder.

I hold my breath just as something tears apart. I'm unsure what happened, but I think a wall in the restroom may have come apart, maybe even the roof, or another part of the building. I hold on tightly as the wind pulls on me, roaring as it rips through the building. The restroom was now full of petrifying screams and the howling wind.

I force myself to look up at the ceiling. At first it was just darkness until a flash of lightning briefly shows my surroundings. Above me I see the ceiling is completely gone.

It returns to darkness once more, and I wasn't quite sure if I was thankful it was so I couldn't see what was happening around me. It felt as this was all a horrible nightmare that I haven't woken up from, but yet I am awake. The smashing, tearing, shattering, roaring, whooping and howling, it was all too much for me. I wanted it all to be over.

Over the roaring and screams, I hear Blake telling me it will be okay and it will soon be over. I can hear it in his voice that he is trying to stay calm for me, hiding the fear in his voice. I can feel his fear as he holds onto me tighter. I can feel the tense of horror in everyone's screams.

It will be over soon, I tell myself repeatedly, but it does nothing to comfort me.

I begin to feel Blake struggling to hang on. Letting go of one hand on the wooden pole that is already starting to feel loosen, and reach out for Blake's arm, hoping I had enough strength to hold him and he will not slip from me.

Something sharp scrapes across my forearm as I just reached out to Blake. I scream, biting down on my lip so hard that I tasted the salted blood in my mouth.

Around me feels bare all of a sudden, like nothing was shielding Blake and me from the wind. When lightning flashes, within a split second I see that the stall walls are gone. The quick flash barely gives me enough time to see my surroundings, but I know the person who was sharing the stall with us is no longer there. I don't hear his screams. Is he dead? Has he been blown away?

Hanging onto the wood made it feel like we were playing a game of tug of war with the tornado. My hand grew tired and sore for hanging on so tightly. My grip began to loosen and I knew the wind was too strong for me to hang on any longer. I could use the other hand, but I couldn't let go of Blake.

Something snaps, and I realise we are no longer on the tile floor. The wooden pole has been pulled out of the tiles. I feel weightless. Blake slips from my grasp.

I may not be able to see what's happening, but when I no longer hear people scream, I know they are either dead or because I know I'm in the air.

As I realise this may be my last breath, my first thought I think about and it's probably my last before I fall onto something hard, is of Mum. Wherever she is right now, I hope she is safe, and that she knows I didn't mean to say the horrible things I had said to her.

Chapter 18

Silence.

I was alive.

But how? I was thrown into the air by a tornado. Why am I not dead? I know there have been stories of people surviving after been thrown, but it all seems surreal to survive such a great fall, especially when travelling at a great speed. I have no idea what strength this tornado was, but most likely it would have been either an EF4 or EF5.

I hear sirens and people screaming out for survivors. I lie there on the ground staring up at the cloudy sky where the rain has stopped. It takes me a moment to remember Blake.

Oh my gosh, Blake!

I sit up in a hurry, and when I do, I feel a sharp pain coming from my right arm as I put pressure on it to sit up. I yelp, fighting back tears that threaten to fall from the intense pain. I can't see in the dark. The moon fights its way out from behind a cloud, only giving me some light to see. I know there is something wrong with my arm, but I can't see. I wasn't sure if that was a good thing, but right now I was glad I couldn't see my surroundings. Later when there will be light, I don't know how I was going to be able to handle seeing the rubble without memories of our vacation flooding back to me.

For a second I'm blinded by a bright light. When I look in the direction where it's coming from, I see the emergency crew setting up flood lights so they are able to see the ruins and search for people who may be trap underneath the rubble.

I glance around me. I forget how to breathe as a lump forms in my throat. Tears swell in my eyes. I have no idea where I am. Everything was unrecognisable. Lucky I wasn't trap beneath the rubble. Every limb of my body aches from hitting the ground hard, but none of the pain compares to the agony that I feel coming from my right arm. When I see the blood and the bone sticking out of my arm, I suddenly feel nausea. My head spins from the sight of the injury. I feel the sickening feeling rising until I can taste the vile in my mouth and vomited.

Wiping my mouth, I stand up, using my good arm to push myself up, which is dripping with blood. I glance at it. The wound is huge and deep that I couldn't look at it at all without feeling nausea.

How the hell did I survive?

I look around, wondering where Blake could be. Where do I look? There is just so much debris that I have no idea how I was going to find him in all of this mess. What if he isn't in the same area as me and was thrown further away from me?

I see some people nearby searching the rubble, as well as emergency crews.

I call out Blake's name, walking around the area. After five minutes I hear someone mumble my name from beneath the rubble. I follow his voice, almost tripping over debris. I soon see a hand sticking out through a hole amongst pieces of wood, twisted metal and pieces of furniture. It's Blake. The tornado had carried him a couple of metres away from where I had landed.

I quickly rush to his aid, ignoring the pain I'm in.

"Blake, are you alright?" I ask. I squeeze his hand with my good one.

"No. I can't move. I think my ribs are broken. I can't breathe without the agony in my chest. I can't move my left arm either. I might have also broken my collarbone. What about you, Charli? Are you hurt?"

"My arm is badly broken. I'm going to move some of this stuff."

Just as I reach for a piece of wood with my good arm, Blake stops me.

"Charli, don't."

"Blake, I need to get you out."

"I know, but you're injured badly. You will injure yourself more if you move any of this, especially on your own. Go get help."

I shake my head. "No, I can't leave you here on your own."

"Charli, listen to me. I will be fine here. Go get help."

I give his hand a quick squeeze, and then carefully made my way through the rubble. I hear a dog barking nearby. About two metres away from where I am standing, I see a group of people searching through the rubble, either for belongings or for survivors. People call out to anyone trapped beneath.

I make my way towards the group. I call out to them, begging for help. A man with glasses and blond hair approaches me to see if I'm alright when he sees my arm and other wounds. Even if I was in so much pain right now, I did not care about myself or the immediate medical attention I needed. I just wanted to make sure Blake gets out safe.

I lead the man and a couple of others to where Blake lies helplessly beneath the rubble. I stand aside as I watch the men move the debris off Blake. Feeling helpless, I move small things with my good arm while the broken one hangs on my side. I cannot move it at all. I bite my lip hard so I don't scream out in agony.

After a few minutes the debris is removed, but the men don't move him in case of spinal injuries. Blake says his back is fine and that he has intense pain in his shoulder and ribs on his left side. One of the men disappears to get the paramedics who are just nearby, assisting someone.

I thank them for their help and then kneel beside Blake.

With his good arm, he reaches out to me and squeezes my hand. "Thank you, Charli."

"Thank goodness you're alright, Blake. I thought we were both going to die."

"I did too, but we were both fortunate."

"What happens now?"

"We will be taken to the hospital."

"What about Mum and Tommy? How do we know they are alright or how would they know where we are?"

He bites down on his lip, fighting back tears. "Once we get to the hospital, I will give them a call. My phone is in my left pocket of my jeans and I cannot move to get it."

I nod. "How far is the hospital from here?"

"It's about an hour away."

I panic at the thought of the hospital being far from here. What if I head to the hospital with Blake while Mum or Tommy is trapped somewhere? Will they be found, especially in the darkness? What if they are being treated at the hospital too and we don't know about it?

I have to find them to make sure they are alright. I need to find Mum and apologise to her for the way I acted towards her. What if they are both out there searching for Blake and I, assuming we are dead when they cannot find us under the rubble when we are at the hospital?

I hear someone telling me to take a deep breath and to breathe slowly, but their voice is dim that I have no idea who is talking. It might have been Blake or one of the men who had helped me. Someone's arms wrap around me, gently placing me on the ground. I want to fight back, telling the person I didn't want to sit at all, not until I find Mum and know she is alright.

I repeatedly tell them I need to find Mum. I need to check to see if the tornado hadn't hit her house. Someone tells me that Mum will be found, and wants to know if she was with me when the tornado occurred. I hear Blake speaking now, he is telling me to keep calm and that once we get to the hospital, he will get in contact with both her and Tommy. I don't want to wait until we get to the hospital. I want to know now if she is alright. Is there a way of reaching for Blake's phone without making his injuries worse if I move him?

My head spins and I'm unable to breath. A paramedic is soon kneeling in front of me while his partner assists Blake. He tells me to breathe slowly, but I can't. There was just too much for me to think about that it made me light-headed, and the pain in my arm doesn't help much as the panic attack continues. Suddenly I'm no longer worry about my broken arm or about Mum. I'm now terrified the tornado will come back for me, taking away everyone I know and love. Although the storm has past, I can still hear the wind and everything smashing and tearing to pieces in my mind.

The last thing I see before I black out is the paramedic's worried expression upon his face, catching me before my head hits the ground.

Chapter 19

Someone calls my name. It sounds like my mother's. When I regain the strength to open my eyes, I stare up at the paramedic with a puzzle look, unsure why he was speaking in my mother's voice. He continues speaking, asking me if I feel pain anywhere else besides my arm. His words confuse me and I had no idea what he was talking about.

It takes me a few minutes to remember everything – the tornado, my broken arm, Blake trapped underneath the rubble, worrying about where Mum could be and whether or not if she was still alive.

I sit up in a hurry, putting pressure on my arm and causing it to ache. I yelp out in pain, tears swelling up in my eyes. I glance down at my arm. It's now in a splint. I hear the paramedic telling me to take deep breaths as my heart rate races. But I couldn't take the deep breaths like he had asked me to. I can hear the sound of the tornado in my mind. Mum is out there somewhere and she doesn't even know if I am alive. I don't even know if she is alive. I visualise the structure of her house in my head, the same way I had memorise her house before Blake and I left her alone. I visualise Mum taking shelter during the storm as the tornado rips apart the house. Where did she take shelter in this violent storm? Perhaps the bathtub since it would have been her only protection from the tornado.

"Charli, Charli, listen to me," I hear Blake's voice calling me.

I close my eyes, listening to his gentle voice as he tells me to stay calm and take keep breaths. He reminds me about the kiss and tells me to picture it in my head. I listen to him, and the kiss instantly takes my mind off everything that has happened. I take in deep breaths and then exhale it slowly, as the happy memory helps me to forget about my phobia.

I breathe normally. With my breathing under control, I look around at my surroundings, realising I was in the back of an ambulance. The paramedic is watching me carefully, asking me again if I was alright. I nod and glance over at Blake, who is lying on the stretcher beside me. His arm is in a sling. He doesn't say anything, just stares at me with a concern look. I thank him for calming me down.

"Do you have any pain anywhere else other than your arm?" the paramedic asks me for what I think is the second or third time, maybe more.

I shake my head. "No. I don't feel any other pain. But I am thirsty. Do you have any water?"

"Sorry, miss, but you won't be able to have any food or water until you have seen a doctor. You may need surgery."

I nod, trying my best to ignore the dryness in my throat. "How long will we be at the hospital?"

The paramedic shrugs. "I can't really tell you. It may be hours, especially with the amount of people coming in with injuries from the tornado."

I turn to Blake. I don't have to say anything. He knows exactly what I'm thinking.

"Once we're settled at the hospital, I will call Tommy. I'm sure your mom is safe with him."

I nod. I lay back on the stretcher, biting my lip as I try to fight back tears.

***

The emergency room is chaotic when we arrive; nurses and doctors were running around helping the injured from the tornado as much as they could. Blake is taken somewhere while I sit and wait to be seen by the doctor. A nurse gives me some morphine to help with the pain. It takes an hour for a doctor to see me. By then I'm so dopey by the drug that all I wanted to do is sleep.

The doctor examines my arm, telling me how bad the break was in my forearm. The compound fracture will need surgery to put it back into place. I thought I would be taken to theatre straight away, but first I had to get x-rays done. I then had to wait for another hour to get in since the theatre was full of people with major injuries.

I wonder where Blake is. He has to be here somewhere. I wonder if he needs surgery for his injuries as well.

***

I have no idea how much time has pass since the doctor took x-rays when I wake up later. The emergency room is still chaotic as more

135

and more people come in. I watch as people come in one by one with all kind of injuries from broken bones to debris cutting open skin. Some had just minor cuts and bruises. I keep an eye out for Mum and Tommy, but I don't see any of them. I try not to think about the worst scenario.

I hear a child scream out in agony. Hearing them takes me back when we were inside the stall, people's petrifying screams as everything tears apart around us. I cover my ears to block out the noise, but it didn't stop the memories. All I can hear is the roaring sounds, something I know I will never forget.

I need to get out of here. I push myself up off the bed, ignoring the slight pain I have in my arm. Thank goodness the morphine has help with most of the pain. I didn't care if my arm was only in a splint, and I still had to wait to fix it in surgery. I have to get out of here and find Mum. I don't know how I'm going to get back to Brennan Heights without a vehicle. Maybe Blake and I could get a hold of Tommy to come get us. If we couldn't then maybe we had to hitch hike, hoping someone would be willing to drive us back to the town.

I walk around the ward, searching for Blake, hoping he wasn't in surgery. It takes me at least ten minutes or more to find him in this chaotic place. He is lying in a bed at the other end of the ward where I was. He had his arm in a sling to support his shoulder as he lies still, his eyes closed.

"Blake?"

He opens his eyes and smiles when he sees me. "Hey, how are you doing?"

"Not so great. All I can think about is my mum. I'm meant to go into surgery to get my arm fix, but don't know how long I need to wait. The longer I wait, the more anxious I feel about her."

Blake taps the edge of the bed beside him with his good hand. "Come sit."

I listen and sit down on the bed. He squeezes my hand.

"Hey, we are going to get out here soon and find her. Maybe she and Tommy will check to see if we show up here."

"I don't know if I can wait for that long. What if she is trapped somewhere and isn't found until daylight? What if by then it's too late?"

"Hey, it's alright. We will get out soon."

"How bad are your injuries?"

"I have a broken collar bone and three broken ribs on my left side. The good thing is they aren't compound fractures so I don't need surgery at all."

"Are you able to call Tommy and my mother?"

He nods. "Could you do me a favour, and grab my phone from that draw beside me? The nurse put my belongings in there."

I get off the bed and open up the draw in the cupboard beside his bed. His clothes were folded neatly in a plastic bag. I untie the knot and take out his phone, and hand it to him. He thanks me and then slides his finger across the screen, clicking contacts. Mum's name is the first on the list. He dials the number, putting it on speaker. I stand there anxiously as I hear the dial tone. It kept on ringing with no one picking up. I feel nausea. Something is wrong.

The dial tone finally ends, cutting to Mum's voice mail. Rather than leaving a message, he hangs up and then scrolls down his list of contacts until he comes to Tommy, pressing his name. He answers on the third ring.

"Oh, thank goodness, Blake," he says. "I was beginning to worry when I couldn't reach you because the signal was down. I'm glad this time the signal is back. Where are you? Are both you and Charli safe?"

He nods. "Yes, we're alright. We are at the hospital over in Kingswood. We were fortunate to survive after being thrown by the tornado. We escaped with some injuries. We may be at the hospital for a while."

"I'm glad you both are alright. I will try and get to you as soon as I can."

"Tommy, have you seen my mum?" I ask him. "Is she alright?"

Tommy is silent for a few minutes. "I'm afraid I can't get in contact with her."

I stop breathing.

"I'm trying to get to her home. The tornado had ripped through her neighbourhood. The emergency crew has the road to her place completely block off. It hit her neighbourhood head on. I'm going to see if I can get there on foot."

"Can you let us know as soon as you find her?" Blake asks.

"I will." He hangs up.

I breath heavily, my chest aching. Mum is missing.

And it's my fault. I shouldn't have left her alone. I should have stayed with her. Maybe then she wouldn't be missing.

I shouldn't have fought with her. Now I may never get the chance to apologise.

I feel Blake's hand on my arm. "Charli, hey. Keep calm. Tommy is going to find her."

"And what if he doesn't? It will be my fault if she is dead!"

Blake shakes his head. "No, it is not your fault and you don't know if she is dead."

"She didn't answer the phone!"

"Yes, maybe she is unconscious, or maybe she is badly injured that she can't move or she is trapped and can't answer it. Maybe she doesn't have her phone on her."

I nod, knowing he was right, but all I can think about is the horrible things I said to her before we left. Will I get a chance to apologise to her? "I was mean to her, Blake. I was so mad at her that I told her to leave me alone."

Blake stares at me for a long time. After a few minutes he says, "Okay. We will get out of here as soon as we can and head back to Brennan Heights. It's not going to be easy getting out or finding a way back to the town, but I'm going to help you find your mom. She is going to be alright, Charli."

I smile at him, hugging him. I accidentally crush him with his sore ribs. Apologising to him, I stroll back to my bed to grab my things before the doctor comes back for me. Right now my arm can wait. I need to find Mum.

Chapter 20

We take our time getting out of the hospital as Blake couldn't move fast enough because of his injury. As we move about in the ward, I was terrified of getting caught leaving the hospital without discharging ourselves. The ward is far too busy for anyone to take notice of us sneaking out.

Once outside, Blake calls for a taxi, and we head to the front entrance to wait. We sit down on a brick wall, sitting in silence as we wait for our ride. I look up at the night sky. It looks as if it may rain again. Hopefully it will just be rain and nothing else. I couldn't bear to see or be in another tornado.

It's half an hour before the driver gets here. I help Blake into the backseat of the taxi. He tells the driver where we wanted to go. The driver looks at us like we were insane for wanting to go anywhere near the disaster zone, but doesn't say anything.

We sit there in silence all through the drive, with only the radio breaking the sound barrier. I bite my lip as I fight back tears as the news reader talks about the tornado. Two different tornadoes touched down in Dante County. Though it was too early to determine the rating, but it's believed an EF3 touched down in another town near Brennan Heights. Although the storm wasn't meant to hit us at all, the storm changed course. The tornado that hit our town was no doubt an EF5.

Oh god, I hope Mum is alright and Tommy has found her.

As we come close to the town, the driver slows down. Up ahead we can see the red and blue flashing lights from emergency vehicles.

"I don't think I'm able to get through at all," the driver tells us. "It looks like the road is completely blocked off."

"You can drop off us here then," Blake says. "We should be able to find our own way from here."

"Are you sure? I can always find another way through the town."

"It's alright. Just let us out here."

Blake goes to reach for his wallet, but winces as he moves. I reach for it in his right pocket and pull out the currency needed to pay the driver.

"Are you sure you want to walk, Blake? It's a long walk to my mother's and your ribs are broken."

"I will be fine. Don't worry about me."

Of course I was worried about him. I have no idea how far my mother's home was from here, but I knew it will take us a while to get there when Blake had to take his time. Did we even have the time to walk slowly? Maybe Tommy has already located her and we didn't have to worry so much about looking for her.

I hand the driver the money and then thanked him for driving us. As we get out of the car, he tells us to take care. He then does a U-turn and disappears back the way we came. We move to the side of the road to get out of the way of any other cars.

Blake takes his good hand into mine and we walk down the street that is full of ruins. A lump forms in my throat as I fight back tears.

Seeing the damage caused by the tornado still seemed surreal, like a terrifying nightmare that I have not yet woken up from. Some buildings were lucky to be still standing, some weren't touched at all, and some had minor damaged while some were completely levelled. People walk around searching through the rubble, either for belongings or for their love ones. I see one young girl, maybe about seven years old, holding onto her teddy bear as she stayed close to her mother, sobbing.

I squeeze Blake's hand tightly. I wonder just how much of this town the tornado destroyed. I wasn't sure if I should be thankful that I don't live in an area where a tornado is more likely to strike. I don't think I could go through what these people in Tornado Alley could go through all the time. But I guess that is the thing about tornadoes. They can strike at anytime, anywhere. Even in an area where you think you will be safe could happen when you at least expect it. They are unpredictable.

I hear a man scream out someone's name. Blake and I turn in the direction of the man's voice. To our left, an African-American man runs towards the woman of the same race. They reunite in each other's arms. I smile at them, as well as others around me as everyone stayed close to their families, friends, neighbours and even strangers. As I watch them, I realise just one thing about this natural disaster is that even if you lose part of your home or become completely homeless, the one thing that matters the most is you're alive as well as your family, friends, neighbours and strangers. I may never have experience anything they may have gone through, but I know that's the one thing I would be grateful the most if I ever lost my home in this disaster.

"Your mom is going to be fine, Charli," Blake tells me.

I nod, biting my lip as we walk. "Yeah."

"Can you do me a favour and reach for my phone? I will call Tommy and see if he has located your mom."

I nod, reaching for his phone in his pocket. I hand it to him, watching him carefully as he scrolls through his contact list and taps Tommy's number. He places it on speaker for both of us to hear. I wait anxiously as his phone keeps ringing. Tommy doesn't pick up until the sixth ring.

"Yes, Blake?"

"Tommy, Charli and I are in Brennan Heights. We are heading to April's place now. Have you found a way to get down her street?"

There's silence on the other end of the receiver. At first I thought maybe the phone got disconnected, but then the uneasy feeling in the pit of my stomach indicated that he was still on the line. He was hesitating about telling us with what was going on. Oh god, please tell me Mum is alright.

"Tommy, are you still there?" I say. "Is my Mum alright?"

"Yes, I am still here, Charli... I don't know what to tell you."

My heart stops beating as my breath is caught in my throat.

He continues on. "I haven't been able to locate her, Charli. There is nothing left of the house either. I have been trying to call her, but all I get is her voice mail."

I lose all feeling in my legs. My knees hit the ground hard as my legs gave way. I hardly take notice of the pain as I break down into tears, my entire body shaking. Blake carefully kneels beside me, wrapping his good arm around me.

"My mum is gone," I mumble through my tears. "I told her that I wanted her to leave me alone."

"Charli, we will find her."

I pull away from Blake. "What if we don't find her?"

Blake wipes away the tears. He stares at me, stroking my face as he tries to find the right words to comfort me with. "I may not be able to promise you anything. I somehow know we will find her. I have never lost anyone in a tornado before, but I have heard of many stories where people are separated during the storm. Whether it ends in good or bad news, you will reunite with her again. If Tommy can't find her, then maybe she is already at a shelter. If she doesn't answer her phone, maybe there is no signal, maybe she doesn't have it with her, or maybe it has been smashed. We will find her, Charli. Trust me."

I nod, biting my lip as I force myself to listen to his words. It wasn't easy telling myself that when I had so many scenarios of what could have happened to my mother running through my head. I didn't even want to think about those scenarios, whether if they were good or bad.

And if we do find her body...? I can't bear to think of an ending for that question.

I guess all I can do right now is think positive, and hope for the best.

Chapter 21

From the moment we are born, I sometimes wonder what our first thought is when the doctor places us into our mother's arms for the first time. You are crying as you gasp for your first breath of air. Your mother cries as soon as she lays her eyes on you for the first time. As soon as you gaze into your mother's eyes, you stop crying as she cuddles you, and you know from that moment on she will always protect you.

I try to think of the earliest memory I could remember of my mother. I don't remember my exact early memory, but one of them I can recall was when I was four. It may not be a great memory, but it's definitely something I would never forget. I ran off from her in the shopping centre. It didn't take long for me to get lost. I cried, fearing I would never see Mum again. A security guard finds me after she reported me missing. He takes my hand and leads me to the central management where Mum was waiting. As soon as she sees me, she races to me with tears of joy, wrapping her arms around me, making me promise her that I would never run off like I did again.

As I gotten older, I never really felt close to Mum, but she was always there when I needed her the most. She was my doctor, my nurse, my teacher, my guidance counsellor; she is everything who

I want her to be. She may not have always been at home when she worked different shifts at the hospital, but she always made time for me, as well as Dad.

Things changed that day when we went on vacation as a family. We never really talked about how we felt after our near death experience with the tornado. It was something we never wanted to remember. Both of my parents were aware of the sudden fear I had of storms. In between their jobs and my mother's studies, I was sent to different therapies to help me deal with that day, but neither of them got any help. I don't know if they were affected by the incident or not, but I guess they dealt with it in their own way. Dad dealt with it without talking, and Mum dealt with it by studying meteorology.

The day Mum left for good after the divorce, I felt lost. There were some days when I thought it was my fault for Mum leaving me. I thought she didn't love me anymore. Dad kept telling me that Mum will always love me no matter what. I try to keep it in mind, but sometimes I didn't want to believe it, not when she wasn't around.

Since arriving here to visit her I have been nothing but a horrible person to her. I have treated her like crap when all she wanted to do was show me that she still cared.

How could I have been so damn selfish?

I'm lost in my own thoughts that I almost didn't hear Blake calling my name, asking me if we could stop to rest for a few minutes. I didn't want to stop until I reach my mother's house, but with his ribs hurting him, Blake needed to take a rest.

After a few minutes rest, we continue on walking. It takes us fifteen minutes to reach Mum's street. Rosewood Street was completely flattened. A few buildings were only just standing, while others weren't so lucky.

"There is basically nothing left of this town," Blake says, his voice croaking. I turn to look at him, watching as he fought back tears. "I have been in a couple of tornadoes. I have been on dozens of chases with Tommy and April. I have seen the damaged these storms can do, but I have never seen it flatten an entire town before."

I take his good hand and squeeze it.

"I wish I have my video camera with me right now," he says. "I could use this footage for my film."

"Charli, Blake?"

My heart skips a beat when I hear his voice. As much as I disliked Tommy for dating my mother, I was thankful to see him when he ran over to us. Before I knew what I was doing, I ran to him. I leap in his arms, hugging him tightly. He must have been startled by my actions, especially when a few hours ago I was mad at him for being with my mum, but right now none of that even matters. It takes him a few minutes to adjust to my actions, and wraps his arms around me, hugging me tightly. I bury my face in his chest, bursting into tears. He pats my hair with one hand as he continues to stand there holding onto me.

"I'm so glad to see you both are okay," Tommy says. He pulls away from me and then carefully hugs Blake.

"What about you, Tommy?" Blake asks. "Are you alright?"

Tommy nods, pulling away. "I'm alright. I was in the motel when it happened. The tornado didn't come anywhere near it."

I began to wonder what would have happened if I hadn't been acting like a total jerk when I had yelled at both Mum and Tommy.

We would probably be staying at a motel in another city, town or state. The four of us would have been together. We would have been safe. But instead I started an argument, and demanded to be taken to the airport so I could have caught the next flight back home. Rather than driving me straight to the airport like I requested, I was taken here to Mum's hometown. If Blake hadn't come over to get me, would I be with Mum right now, trap underneath the rubble?

"Does April have a storm shelter?" Blake asks as Tommy leads us to where Mum's house once stood.

"Yes, she does. The shelter is inside the garage, but she isn't in there." He stops and turns to the both of us. "I thought that's where she might have been, but she wasn't. I somehow have a feeling that she wasn't inside the house at all when the tornado hit."

I feel my stomach twisting into knots, making me feel nausea. "What do you mean she wasn't in the shelter? Of course she was, wasn't she?"

Tommy shrugs. He fought back tears. "Her car isn't around. I have no idea how far the tornado could have thrown it, but I can't find it anywhere in this area. She was on the phone with me, telling me she was on the way to the motel. I told her to stay where she was to be safe, but I have no idea if she was driving while she was on the phone. Her phone cut out while I was speaking to her."

I couldn't think. I couldn't breathe.

"But why would she be driving to the motel to reach you?" Blake asks. "Why didn't she take shelter?"

"She called me to ask if I knew where you two were. She was going to come get you both and take you to the motel. Even though the weather reports were saying the storm wasn't to come anywhere near our town, she somehow knew the storm was going to change course. She tried to call you, Blake, but she couldn't reach you."

Blake looks at him, surprised. "Really? I didn't hear it ring."

"That's when she called me, asking if I knew where you both were. I told her to stay at the house where she can get to shelter if the tornado was to come our way. I-I don't know what happened. All I heard on the phone was this loud crash and April screaming before the phone cut off. I then called you, but our phones had a bad connection."

My breathing gets worse as my chest gets tighter, making it feel like I was having a heart attack. Mum was out there somewhere. She was out there because of me. She could be anywhere. She could be lying in a ditch somewhere, dead, but that's something I didn't want to even think about.

"It's my fault that she is out there!" I cried as I collapse to my knees. "She could be dead because of me! I told her to leave me alone, and that's what she did!"

Tommy kneels beside me and makes me look at him. "Charli, listen to me. Don't you dare blame yourself for your mother's disappearance. It's not your fault. It's no one's fault. Your mom was concerned about your safety. That's why she came after you and Blake. She risked her own life to make sure you both were safe."

I think back to when Blake told me the real reason why Mum left Dad and me to pursue her dream in meteorology. Sometimes I wonder why she never told us that she was terrified of losing us both through the storm. Maybe like Dad and me, we never told each other how we really felt after the tornado. We kept things

149

to ourselves. Her way of distracting herself from what happened was to study and chase tornadoes in the mid-west of America. Saving lives was something Mum had always wanted to do when she was working as a nurse. As much as I think that this whole job about chasing tornadoes is stupid, I realise now it isn't. If it wasn't for storm chasers like Mum and Tommy, lives wouldn't be saved if there weren't warnings. Storm chasers dedicated their lives to assure people are safe and can get to safety in time.

And even though she knew the risk of driving during the night with a tornado warning, she sacrificed her life to make sure Blake and I was in a safe place. There was no warning of an approaching tornado until it was right near us. Maybe if it was during the day we would have been okay, but it wasn't, and that's what made it harder to know that the funnel was on the ground.

Even if there was no tornado warning for our town, only for other towns nearby, no one could have predicted that it was going to come our way. Mum somehow had a feeling the storm was going to change course even though the weather reports said it wouldn't.

And I failed to listen to her warnings, as well as Blake. If we had stayed with her, we would have been safe in the shelter. I had panicked too much that I never asked if she had a storm shelter.

"Listen, Charli," Tommy continues on, "it's getting late. Why don't I take you and Blake to a shelter where you can get some sleep? I will continue looking for your mom."

I shake my head. "No. I'm not going to some shelter or even a hospital while you search for my mum. I know that right now I need to get my arm fixed in surgery, but I do not care about it right now. My arm is in a splint so it should keep the bone in place until I do get surgery done. I can't lie in a hospital bed without knowing whether or not if my mother is alive. I need to find her, Tommy. I'm coming with you."

He nods. "Okay. You can come with me." He turns to Blake. "Do you think you can continue walking, or do you want to go and settle into a shelter for the night?"

"I may have to stop and rest, but I'm going to help you find April too," Blake says.

Chapter 22

It's almost midnight. We have been wandering around for hours in hope of finding my mother, but all we got was exhaustion and sore feet. We stopped a few times for Blake to rest. I don't mean to sound so impatient waiting for him, and I knew how much pain he was in with his injuries right now, but the more I waited while searching for my mother, the more anxious I felt in wondering where she could be.

We stop to take a longer break this time to give our exhausting bodies a chance to rest from all of the walking. It also gave us time to think where my mother could be rather than just guessing where she might be. As much as Tommy wanted to keep looking for Mum, he was worried about Blake and me, especially for Blake. He wondered if all of this walking was too much for him. He suggested for the second time that Blake and me should head to the shelter to rest for the night while he kept searching, but there was no way I was doing that. I couldn't let him search for her on his own. Even a few emergency crew workers suggested we turn in for the night. I drag my body along, not even knowing how I could sleep at all. I had to find her because by morning it could be too late.

Tommy makes Blake and me to take a seat on a mattress. I don't listen to his request and remain standing as Blake lies down rather than sit. Tommy then tells us to stay where we were so he could search for some water.

"You can sit down beside me, Charli," Blake says. "There is enough room for the both of us."

I look down at him. He was right. There is enough room for us to lie down on the Queen-size mattress, but I felt as if Blake needs it more than me. "I'm fine, Blake."

"Stop lying to yourself and sit down. Rest your feet."

"What about you, Blake? You are injured more than me. You can't even sit up and walk without having difficulty breathing because of your ribs."

"Yes, it's hard to breath or even move, but I'm honestly fine. You can choose to lie down with me or you can sit. It's up to you. Either way your feet are killing you. I don't know how long we are going to sit here for or how much further we are going to be walking for, but you might as well as take an advantage of resting here because who knows how long we will be here for or how much further we will have to walk."

I listen to him, knowing he was right. I look over at Tommy to see him moving some debris among the rubble near a refrigerator. I turn back to Blake and carefully lie down beside him. We lie there in silence, being careful not to touch each other where our injuries were.

Everything is quiet except for a few people nearby calling out to people who are still trapped from underneath the rubble. The sky is clear with the stars shining brightly. The moon is hidden behind a cloud. I wonder to myself if the worst is over.

"How's your arm?" Blake asks me. "Are you still in a lot of pain?"

I nod as I turn to him. "It hurts, but I'm trying not to focus on the pain. How about you?"

"Well, all I can say is that breathing slowly is not very easy when you are trying to keep your rib cage still. Charli, can you promise me something once we find your mother?"

"Sure."

"Promise me you will get your arm look at. Right now it's in a splint and it will be kept stabilise to prevent more injury, but I'm not sure how long you can have it in a splint for. Maybe for a couple of days, but eventually you will need to fix the bone or it will never heal. I understand how much you really want to find your mom, but you also need to take care of yourself."

I nod, knowing he was right. I should have done that in the first place and went through surgery, but I had no idea how long I would have to wait for or how long I would be in recovery. Mum could have minutes to live wherever she is. She could be trap somewhere that no one knows about. Emergency crew would most likely search for survivors in popular areas first before looking somewhere they would at least expect a person to be.

I turn away from him and glance up at the sky again. I concentrated on the stars, trying to think positive as Blake and I lie there in silence. After a few minutes of just lying there and thinking, my eye lids grow heavy. I fight to keep them open, not wanting to close them until I have found my mother.

Before my eye lids had the chance to win, Tommy comes back with a bottle of water for us to share. I sit up and drank enough to sooth my dry throat. Tommy then helps Blake to sit up so he could have some of the drink too.

"We need to go back the way we came," Tommy tells us. "The road is block off because of live wire all over the road."

"So where are we going to look for April now?" Blake asks, handing the bottle back to Tommy.

Tommy takes the bottle and screws the lid back on. "I have no idea. She could have been anywhere during the storm."

"You are definitely certain she was driving when she called you?" I ask him.

"I'm positive."

"When you called me at the restaurant, how long ago did you speak to April?" Blake asks.

Tommy thinks for a second. "Maybe about four to five minutes."

"Okay, let's try and narrow this down to where she could be rather than just guessing and wasting time finding her. The restaurant is about eight blocks northeast from where April lives. So most likely she wasn't far from us if the phone call you made between us is about four to five minutes."

My stomach twists into knots as I put the pieces of Blake's words together, wondering where she could possibly be. It wasn't easy picturing the map of the town in my head, especially when I didn't know Brennan Heights at all.

I think about the little knowledge I knew about tornadoes. I didn't understand the science stuff, but I knew what they are capable of doing. Most people are killed by trying to outrun the tornado in their cars, or sometimes if the funnel is rain wrap, they are caught in it. Depending on the strength of the tornado, it could flip or even toss a vehicle. Escaping alive from the wreckage would be pure luck.

"If she was toss inside her car, how would she survive?" I ask.

Tommy and Blake doesn't answer me straight away. They don't even make eye contact with me. They stare at each other, unsure how they would answer my question.

"Please tell me we have a chance of finding her alive," I say when the guys don't give me an answer at all.

Tommy turns to me, a mix of sadness, hope and worry in his eyes. "I cannot promise you anything, Charli. All we can do is hope she is fine. Yes, if she was thrown from her car there is a high chance she wouldn't have survived. It will be pure luck if she does live."

"So where do you think it's best to look?" I ask.

Tommy turns to Blake. "What do you think, Blake? Should we keep looking around here or try near the area she could have been during the tornado?"

"Well, it will be all depending which way the winds blew her," Blake says. "So far we have been looking around her neighbourhood and to the south. Maybe we could head north, possibly the north west area I reckon she could be."

Tommy agreed it would be a great idea for us to look in that direction. We carry on, heading in the north west direction. Hopefully the things Blake had said were true. Tommy gives my mother's mobile another call, only once again getting her voice mail.

With the lack of sleep, my body was beginning to feel like a zombie as I drag myself along, looking around and calling out to Mum, hoping she was somewhere around here and not too far off.

"Are you folks alright?" an emergency vehicle pulls up alongside us. A man in his forties with short hair and glasses sat behind the wheel. "Do you need any help at all?"

Tommy looks over at Blake and I, seeing the fatigue in us. He turns back to the driver. "Yes, please. We are trying to look for someone, but we aren't sure if we should keep looking. We are all pretty much exhausted from walking."

"Hop in. I can help you out if you like, and if you want me to I can take you guys to the shelter where you can turn in for the night. You can resume your search in the morning. And hopefully the person you are looking for is back at the shelter waiting for you, or if they haven't made it there, the emergency services will find them."

Tommy thanks the driver who introduces himself as Tony. Tommy first helps Blake into the backseat before giving me a hand to get in as well before he joins Tony in the front seat. He drives through the street, being careful of any fallen debris blocking the road. The car gently rocks me to sleep, and I had to strain to keep my eyes open.

"Do you have any idea where this person you're looking for might be?" Tony asks.

"Not really," Tommy says, glancing out the window. "I'm only guessing where she might be. She called me about four to five minutes before the storm hit Blake and Charli, where she was coming to get them. We think she might be north west from here."

"So she was driving when the tornado hit?"

Tommy nods, turning to Tony. "I think she might have been. I couldn't find her in her storm shelter where her house has been demolished. I have tried calling her cell, but all I get is her voice mail."

"We will find her. I'm sure she is safe somewhere."

"Tommy, do you think there would be a chance she might be near the railway?" Blake asks. "I'm thinking that's one of the locations she could be while she was driving before the tornado hit Charli and me."

Tommy looks over at us. "She could be." He turns to Tony. "Do you think we can drive over to the railway and look around there?"

Tony agrees, continuing in the north west direction. Demolished buildings were right along the tracks. Emergency crews were helping some people who was looking for someone or who were trapped beneath the rubble. Tony pulls over so we could get out and have a better look around the area.

We wonder around, calling out to Mum. Blake walks with me while Tommy is with Tony. I wanted to go onto the tracks and see what was there, but it meant climbing over the rubble and there wasn't a clear way for Blake to walk through without injuring himself more.

Just when I thought there was no use in finding her in the mess, Tommy screams out her name. Blake and I turn to him, seeing him climb over the rubble, slipping, cursing as he gets to his feet. Tony is on his heels.

Chapter 23

Blake tells me to go while he waited for us to return with my mother on the street. I was concerned about leaving him behind, but I wanted to see my mother. Maybe he will find another way to get down to the tracks without climbing over obstacles, and injuring himself more.

"April, can you hear me?" I hear Tommy calling out.

I carefully climb over the rubble, almost losing my balance on an unstable surface. I make it to the ground safely to what was left of the backyard of the property I was standing on. Thankfully the houses that once stood on this block of land weren't on a hill that I would have to climb down to get onto the tracks. I hurry over to where Tony and Tommy were standing beside what was left of a red crumpled car.

As I near Tommy, I hear her voice, letting Tommy know that she was alright. My heart stops beating and a lump forms in my throat as I fight back tears. She is alive, just like Blake had promised me she will be. She sounds exhausted and fighting back pain.

"Are you hurt, April?" Tommy asks her.

She squeezes her eyes shut. "I have severe chest pains, and my legs are crushed underneath the dashboard. The steering wheel is also crushing my thighs. My neck is sore as well, but I don't think it's broken. My left shoulder also hurts."

I reach Tommy and stand beside him. He stands aside so I could see her. She is strapped in her seat, dry blood that had been dripping down her face from a cut on her forehead. She turns her head when she sees me, her face lighting up with happiness as soon as her eyes lay on me.

Without saying any words to each other, Mum opens her arms for me. Leaning on the car door, I carefully wrap my arms around her, being careful not to crush any of her injuries. She hugs me tightly as we cry into each other's shoulders. The dispute we had earlier was forgotten. All that matters now is we still had each other.

I pull away from her just as Tony tells us he is going to call for backup.

"Where is Blake?" she asks. "Is he safe?"

I nod. "Yes, he is. He is just on the street."

"Were you both safe from the tornado?"

I recall the terrifying moment in my head. It was something I couldn't repeat without breaking into tears. And right now crying about it wasn't going to help get my mother out of the car.

But lucky for me, Tommy saved me from saying a word. He rests a hand on my shoulders. "They both escaped with injuries, but if I hadn't warned Blake, the seconds I spared them could have been worst if I hadn't managed to get a hold of him."

I think back to when Blake and I were huddled in the restaurant's bathroom with the other customers. I wonder what happened to the others. Did they make it through the storm as well? Were they as lucky as Blake and I?

Mum smiles, hiding her pain behind it. "Thank you, Tommy."

***

I stand by watching as Mum was rescued from the car. It takes the emergency crew at least an hour to free her from it. Before they could start drilling their tools through the wreckage in order to free her, they had to get the okay from the fire brigade to make sure if it was safe enough in case any petrol was leaking.

She was place on a stretcher, fitted with a neck brace for precaution in case of a neck injury. Tommy and I walk alongside her as she was carried to the ambulance. Blake was waiting beside it. As soon as I see him, I left my mother's side and hurry over to him, wrapping my arms around him into a hug.

"My mother's alive, just like you said she will be," I tell him.

"And she is quite fortunate to have survived inside a car," he says, pulling away from me. "Not many people are quite so lucky."

"Charli, do you want to ride in the ambulance with your mother?" Tommy asks me.

"What about you and Blake?" I ask.

"Tony has offered to drive us to the hospital. Why don't you go to the hospital with her and we will meet you there?"

I agree to go and climb into the back of the ambulance with her, although I didn't really know why I went. Mum and I didn't speak at all on the way to the hospital. Mostly she was speaking to the paramedic who was treating her for her injuries. He kept telling her how she was lucky to be alive, especially when not many people do when they try to outrun a tornado in their vehicles.

They continued talking about the storm while I sat there listening, feeling invisible. The paramedic did talk to me, asking me if I was alright and what I was doing during the storm. I answer him, but mostly kept quiet about the tornado. I didn't want to speak of it at all. Mostly all I wanted was to be alone with Mum and apologise to her for my disrespectful attitude towards her.

Once at the hospital, we are separated as she is taken to x-ray to see if she needed surgery. I stay in the waiting room, which is packed and there are no seats for me to sit down. The TV is on, broadcasting the tornado incident. That's when I realise that I need to call Dad and inform him that both Mum and I are alright.

I walk outside so I could get some privacy and press Dad's number on my contact list. My battery still had a fair bit of life left, about forty percent. One phone call should be alright to make while I save the rest of the battery. I have no idea when I will be able to find my luggage amongst the rubble where my charging cord is.

Dad answers almost instantly. "Charli?"

"Hi, Dad.

Chapter 24

When the sun came up in the morning, seeing how calm the sky was you would never had expected during the night a powerful tornado had rip through a small town, injuring hundreds and killing several people. I haven't heard anything on the latest news on the tornado yet.

I lay in the bed I was given after the surgery I needed for my arm, staring out the window, thinking about last night. I haven't been able to check on my mother since we arrived in the emergency ward. I was taken into surgery around four in the morning. The morphine that was flowing through a tube and into my body took away the pain I had to put up with mostly during the night from not going into surgery straight away when I was meant to rather than searching for Mum.

The door opens, interrupting my thoughts. I turn to see Blake walking in with a plastic cup in his hand.

"Oh hey, you're awake." He walks over to me, taking a sip of his drink. "How did you sleep?"

"Alright. Did you get any sleep?"

He takes a seat in a chair beside me. "I had some sleep, but sleeping in a chair is very uncomfortable, especially when you have broken ribs. Would you like some water?"

I nod as I push myself in a sitting position with my good arm. "Yes, please."

Blake hands me his cup and I take a sip. He watches me carefully as I gulp it down.

"What time is it?" I hand the cup back to him.

"It's almost noon. You slept a fair bit after surgery, which went well. Would you like me to go and alert a nurse that you're awake?"

I give him a small smile. "That would be great. Thanks, Blake."

He gets up and heads towards the door.

Before he leaves the room, I call out his name. He turns back to me.

"How is my mother doing?" I ask.

Blake nods, giving me a smile. "She is good. She is lucky is all I can say. She has broken ribs, which was caused when the airbag opened up. She also has a strain shoulder, crushed both of her legs from the dashboard. The luckiest thing about her injuries is her neck. She could have broken it, but instead she bruised it. She's lucky the car rolled, and wasn't toss. It could have been worse if she was toss."

I stare at him, speechless. I couldn't believe the injuries my mother had gotten. I would have expected Blake and I to have more after being thrown in the air. Maybe it was the way we had landed.

I think back to when my family first encounter a tornado. We were so damn lucky to escape with no injuries. This time Mum and I haven't been so fortunate. We may have survived, and I guess that's the main thing, but our injuries could affect our lives forever. This day is something we could never forget.

But the most important thing about this day is that we still have each other.

Thinking about Mum and the injuries Blake had mentioned brought tears to my eyes. I have no idea if what we have been through last night really was a dose of pure luck, but I was thankful to still have Mum with me despite the things we had said earlier to each other. None of it even matters now, although I would have never forgiven myself for acting like a selfish jerk if Mum did die. I may have been mad at her for so many things, but I still wanted her apart of my life. I couldn't live without her.

Blake is soon at my side, pulling me into a hug. "Hey, it's okay. Everything is fine, Charli. We are all safe."

"I know." I pull away from him, wiping my eyes. "I'm just so thankful my mum is alright."

"I told you she will be."

"I know. I just can't imagine what would have happened if we weren't fighting. We would have been safe inside the storm shelter."

Blake touches my cheek with his hand. "Try and not think about what could have happened. None of that matters now. What matters is that you're both alive."

I smile at him, knowing he is right. I place my hand behind his neck and gently push him forward, brushing my lips against his.

He pulls away and then leaves the room to find a nurse to let them know I was awake. An African-American nurse walks in, asking me how I was feeling. I told her I was fine and really wanted to see my mother. She said she will check with the doctor to see if I could see her.

Blake stays with me. It didn't take long for a doctor to walk in, asking me how I was feeling and had a look at my arm. He allows me to see my mother, promising to return later to check on me after seeing other patients.

Lunch was soon served. I didn't have much of an appetite, but Blake made me eat half of the egg and mayo sandwich that's on the tray, while he eats the other half.

We walk slowly through the corridors, taking the lift to the third floor. There wasn't enough room in the emergency room as more injured people were brought in, especially those who weren't found during the night but were found once it was daylight.

I still can't believe how fortunate I have been, as well for Blake and my mother.

Tommy was sitting beside Mum's bed when we walked in, chatting about last night as he delivers the latest news to her. As soon as I see Mum I wanted to burst into tears, but I manage to hold them back. I have cried enough last night and it wasn't going to help Mum get better. She had a bandage wrapped around her head for the wound on her forehead, and both of her legs were elevated.

Mum looks our way and smile. "Hey, how are you two doing?"

Blake walks over to her. I follow right behind him, standing at the foot of my mother's bed. "Still sore from the double amount of pain from both my collarbone and ribs, but other than that I'm fine."

"How are you feeling, Mum?" I ask her.

"Good to be alive," she says with a smile.

"Tommy, do you think you can come back with me to the motel?" Blake asks. "I want to get my camera and shoot some of the damage from last night. I might use it for my film."

"Yeah, sure I can do that." Tommy turns to Mum. "Will you be alright while I'm gone, honey?"

Mum smiles at him. "I will be fine. You go with Blake and help him with the filming." She turns to Blake. "How's the film coming along?"

"It's great," he replies. "It's almost finished and I just hope I have enough footage since we won't be doing anymore chasing for a while. Plus, I'm not going to be able to film really well with one arm."

"Don't worry, buddy," Tommy says as he walks over to him. "I will help you with the filming. Storm chasing may be over for us this season, but we will be able to chase next season."

My stomach twists into knots when Tommy mentioned about next season. How can he and Mum even think of continuing to chase after what happened?

The guys leave the room, leaving me alone with Mum. The two of us were silent. I had great difficulty glancing at my mother, keeping my eyes on the floor. I couldn't look at her. I couldn't see the pain hiding in her eyes. Looking at her made too many memories of the tornadoes come back to me.

"So are you still going to chase tornadoes?" I ask, still not looking at her. I may not be here the next time she chases, but I most definitely didn't want to watch the news, wondering whether or not if Mum was caught in a storm that has destroyed an entire town or city.

"Come sit down, Charli," Mum says.

I listened and sit down in the chair Tommy was previously sitting in. Mum reaches over and pats my knee.

"Honey, look at me."

I do.

"Yes, I will be still chasing tornadoes next season once my injuries heal."

"But why, Mum? You were almost killed."

"Chasing storms is my job."

"It doesn't have to be. You could go back to doing nursing."

"Charli, I know you're worried about what could happen to me. I worry all the time for mine and Tommy's safety. When Blake is with us, our main concern is his safety rather than ours. Yes, you're right. It doesn't have to be my job, and I could go back to doing nursing if I want. But I have left nursing behind so I could study meteorology. Chasing storms is my life now. I want to be able to chase and study them. Tornadoes fascinate me. They are so incredibly amazing when they are on the ground and moving across the land. I only find them amazing when they are out on an open field, away from towns and any property that could be destroyed. It's a risky job, and I know you don't understand why I'm doing this. I'm doing this because I love you. That day when I could have lost both you and your father while we were on vacation made me want to help others. Storm chasers study tornadoes and warn people to get to safety."

I sit there staring at my mother, unsure what I was supposed to say or how to react. She stares back at me, waiting for me to say something, her eyes pleading with me to understand her and to forgive her for leaving me and Dad.

I get up from my chair, leaning down to give my mother a hug, being careful of her injuries.

"I love you, Mum. I'm so sorry for how I have treated you."

Mum kisses my head as she gently rubs my back. "I love you too, sweetie. I always will, you know that don't you?"

I pull away from her. "I know. Dad kept telling me you did, even though I didn't want to believe it when you left."

"I'm sorry for ever making you feel that way. I shouldn't have left you like that, and I'm sorry."

I then let the words I never would have thought of saying slip out of my mouth. "I forgive you, Mum. I'm just so thankful that you're going to be alright. I don't know what I would have done if I had lost you for good."

Mum gives me a warm smile. "I'm thankful that you're alright too."

I sit back down.

"Are you going to be leaving for Sydney soon like you said you wanted to yesterday afternoon?"

I shrug, not really sure if I wanted to leave just yet. I couldn't leave Mum after what happened. And even if I could, I didn't have my passport. Before I can even leave for Sydney I would have to search for my luggage beneath the rubble, and right now I don't think I could visit the wreckage to search for it. "I don't know just yet. I contacted Dad last night to let him know we were both alright. He is leaving today to come here. I don't know how long he will be staying for."

Mum nods, unsure about seeing my dad. "Charli, I can understand if you don't want to visit me again after what happened in the last few days. If you want to leave with your father, I'm okay with it. I just want you to know that I love you, and I should have done more things with you instead of working. I'm sorry. I can understand if you want to say no to this, but I would like you to come back in November to attend Tommy and my wedding."

I smile at her. After Tommy helped me find her, the least I could do in return was agree to attend the wedding.

Chapter 25

The doctor discharged Blake and me by the afternoon, but neither of us leaves the hospital. Tommy had suggested for us to go back to the motel and rest there so we weren't hanging around, while he stays with Mum who couldn't leave for a few more days. I couldn't leave her. Even though she was fine, but I feared that something could happen if I wasn't there. Besides, heading back to the motel meant driving past the ruins of Brennan Heights, and I wasn't prepared to see the damage in broad daylight. There weren't many comfortable places for us to sleep while at the hospital. The only place we could sleep on was chairs that were plastic and uncomfortable in my mother's room.

Sometimes when I'm supposed to be sleeping, I would wake up and hear Tommy and my mother talking. They talked a lot about the future for them and what they are going to be doing for next season, especially when they now no longer had a car. Mostly the money they spent went on their wedding and Mum wasn't sure how they would save for a new SUV. Tommy told her not to worry too much about it and that they will find a way to buy it, even if they weren't able to make an investment with turning their storm chasing vehicle into armour where they would be able to intercept a tornado safely like they originally planned.

I watch them with weary eyes as they continued talking without knowing I was awake. Tommy holds Mum's hand while they talked. I still didn't like the idea of him becoming my step dad, and seeing him where my dad is supposed to be standing crushed my heart. For years I have witnessed how much my parents really did care for each other, and after the incident happened, things began to change. They were no longer the loving couple I remembered growing up with. They were strangers now. I didn't know Tommy well, but the only thing I wanted was for him to treat my mother the same way Dad did.

In the morning I receive a text from Dad that he was in L.A. and was waiting for a flight to Denver. From there he will be hiring a car to drive out this way, most likely arriving here by late afternoon or at night. By the late afternoon, Blake sat with me on a bench outside the main entrance of the hospital, waiting for Dad to arrive.

It's not until sunset when I spot dad walking through the car park towards the main entrance. I leap off the bench and ran towards him, leaping into his arms. Dad hugs me tightly, like he was terrified of letting me go.

"I'm so glad you are alright, Charli," he says. "As soon as I heard about the tornado, I didn't think at first that you would be anywhere near it, and then I remembered that your mother lived in Brennan Heights." He pulls away from me. "How is your mother doing?"

I tell him about Mum's condition. He curses softly under his breath.

Blake comes over to us. I introduce Dad to him, who thanks Blake for doing his best to keep me safe from the tornado. He then follows us to Mum's room.

We reach the room and Dad just stands at the door rather than going in. He stares at my mother who hadn't taken notice that the three of us had walked in. Tommy was standing beside her bed as she hands him a bottle of water to place on the bedside table.

"April?"

Mum and Tommy glance our way.

"Ian."

There's silence as Mum and Dad stare at each other for a long time. After a while Dad walks over and hugs her.

***

After a few days Mum was finally released from the hospital. Tommy had offered Dad and me to stay at his house in Dale so we didn't have to stay in a motel. At first Dad wasn't sure whether or not if it was a good idea if the three of us was to stay in the same house, especially with any tension that could build up between him and Mum. Luckily we were only staying at the house for two days before heading back home to Sydney.

On the last night before we head home, Blake came over to spend his last moment with me. We sat on the back verandah, watching the storm that was over us. I wanted to go inside, but he wanted me to stay outside. I was worried about another tornado, but Blake assured me that the storm wasn't a supercell. The sound of the rain pattering down relaxes me a little, but the thunder wasn't helping much.

"So you're definitely going to be back for your mother's wedding?" Blake asks me.

I nod. "Yes I am. I'm still not sure about Tommy being my stepfather, especially when I haven't known him for so long."

"Maybe when you come for the wedding you could stay longer and get to know him."

"I will see."

A flash of lightning rips across the sky. I squeeze Blake's good hand tightly that I have been holding onto since the storm started. Thunder rumbles.

Blake chuckles. "You're never going to get over your fear of storms, are you?"

I let go of his hand and gently slap him on his good arm. "Hey, it's not funny." I stick my tongue out at him.

"You're right. I shouldn't laugh. I'm sorry. I should just be happy that you're out here with me and not hiding somewhere crying."

I chew on my lip as I nod; surprised I wasn't doing the same thing. "You have no idea how much I want to run inside right now and hide."

Blake takes my hand again. "How are you feeling right now?"

As he mentions it, there's another flash of lightning. I squeeze his hand as thunder rumbles. I take a deep breathe.

"Truthfully I really want to throw up right now," I answer his question. "I'm trying to stay calm as much as I can so I don't have a panic attack. You have helped me to stay calm more than what therapy has ever helped."

He smiles at me. "I'm glad to help."

I return the smile and then move closer to him, leaning in to kiss him. Blake slowly turns in a comfortable position and leans in the rest of the way. With his good hand, he places it on my jaw. For a moment I forget about the storm until the sound of thunder made me jump, pulling away from Blake.

"I really think we should go inside, Blake," I tell him, worried the storm may be getting worse.

Blake pushes my hair away from my face and tucks it behind my ear. "Relax, Charli. We are fine out here."

I nod, taking a deep breath.

"Can you promise me something, Charli?"

"Sure."

"I know how terrified you are of storms, but please promised me you will visit next season to chase tornadoes with us. If you come and stay longer, spend the whole season with us, maybe it will help you with your fear this time more than what it has in the last few days when you arrived here."

I stare at him, surprised he was asking me to continue chasing tornadoes. It wasn't something I was planning to do next year. I still wasn't even sure how chasing tornadoes could help conquer my fear of storms, especially with what we have just been through. People always tell me in order to conquer my fear, I need to face it. The phobia will always be there. I just need to learn how to control my panic attacks more.

I give Blake a warm smile, promising him I will join the chase next season before leaning forward to kiss him again.

Want more storm chasing adventures? Check out the next book in
the *Storm Chasers* series

Chasing Tornadoes

Anna and Jeremy love storm chasing together. While Jeremy
studied the science side, Anna photographs them. But one spring
day, a storm chase goes wrong. An EF4 tornado almost wipes out
their hometown. Jeremy is killed, leaving Anna to wonder what
had gone wrong.

When Anna is offered to go on a chase with Jeremy's cousins, she
is unsure at first. How could she chase without her best friend?
Without Jeremy, she probably would never have chased tornadoes.
Her friend Moxie convinces her to never stop doing what she and
Jeremy loved the most. Chasing with Jeremy's cousins who also
storm chase might help Anna to move on and to figure out what
she wants as a storm photographer.

Acknowledgments

This story was one I enjoyed writing. It was a challenge with a constant research, especially when I have never seen or been in a tornado before. I think I spent more time watching documentaries on them, along with the movies *Twister* and *Into the Storm* than actually writing this.

Tornadoes have always been a fascination to me from the very first time I watched the movie *Twister* when I was six or seven years old. Despite the destruction they leave, I always found them fascinating how they formed and moved. I always find tornadoes at their best when they are in the middle of nowhere, away from anything they can destroy.

This story inspired me from some of my favourite storm chasers like Reed Timmer, who is known for the Dominator. Storm chasers put their lives at risk every time, getting all of the data and anything that helps them to understand more about tornadoes, and helping communities get to safety. And this story is dedicated to them all, especially to Tim and Paul Samaras, and Carl Young who lost their lives in the El Reno, Oklahoma 2013 tornado.

And now to thank a few people who helped with the encouragement for this story. Thank you to my sister Jennifer Madden for putting up with my obsession with *Into the Storm*, who thought I was insane when I chose to watch it almost every day when it was first released on DVD. Thank you also to Tammy Nickell who helped me a little on research with knowing what it was like to be in Tornado Alley when the sirens go off, which also helped me to understand my character Charli better with her fear of storms. Thank you to Sarah Swartz for the awesome Wattpad trailer she made for this book. Thank you also to Melissa Rodriguez for sharing your story with me about being one of the students trapped in the rubble of the Plaza Towers Elementary School of the Moore, Oklahoma 2013 tornado. Lastly, thank you to Heather Landskro, who has been a huge supporter with this story on Wattpad. You were the one who really encouraged me to get this book published, and to share Charli's story to the world.

About the Author

Jessica Madden was born and raised in Sydney, Australia. She began writing stories since the age of eight. When she was nine, she realised that she wanted to be a writer more than anything in the world. At twenty-three years old, Jessica published her first book *Right Here Waiting for You*. Writing about characters falling in love has always been her favourite thing to write about.

When she is not writing, Jessica is often daydreaming up new storylines, and can be found lost in reading a good book.

You can follow her on Instagram and X @JessicaCMadden

You can also subscribe to her newsletter at https://mailchi.mp/262f0baec4df/books-writing-and-my-writer s-life

Also by Jessica Madden

Right Here Waiting For You
The Jet Lag Diaries
Silent Love
If You Had Stayed
Hating Jamie Jackson
This Song Is For You

I Wasn't Supposed To Fall For You

I Wasn't Supposed To Fall For You
It's All Because of You

Storm Chasers

Chasing the Storm
Chasing Tornadoes

With You

One Whole Night With You
Every Moment With You

www.ingramcontent.com/pod-product-compliance
Lightning Source LLC
Chambersburg PA
CBHW030635120726
47904CB00006B/2158